PRAISE

FOR DOMENIC STANSBERRY

On **THE WHITE DEVIL** (recipient of Hammett Prize)

Edgar-winner Stansberry takes the reader on a wild ride in this exceptional noir ... Compelling Reading. —**Publishers Weekly** (Starred Review)

A glittering noir triumph ... Recounted in a delirious, shimmeringly erotic flow, The White Devil *is a possessed, fever dream of a book, an unwise third cocktail that proves impossible to resist.* —**The Irish Times**

Gripping from beginning to end, The White Devil *is an unforgettable novel by an author at the height of his powers.* —**Foreword Reviews**

Erotic and sophisticated. —**Sunday Times (UK)** Top 10 Summer Crime Club Selection

With its down-to-the-bone, spare prose style ... and scenes that would not be out of place in a Fellini classic, The White Devil *is quite simply perfect in its execution.* —**UK Raven Crime**

On **THE CONFESSION** (recipient of Edgar Award)

In the literary tradition of The Killer Inside Me, *and every bit as powerful ... Stansberry is an extraordinarily evocative writer.* —**George Pelecanos,** writer/producer *The Wire*

A masterful novel by a (heretofore) under appreciated master of the genre. Very highly recommended. —**Bookreporter.com**

Fabulous writing, excellent pace and a thoroughly unnerving unreliable narrator results in a book that sticks in your craw, your brain and your gut for a very long time. —**Sarah Weinman,** Confessions of an Idiosyncratic Mind

This first-person account will give you goosebumps for days. .... With masterful technique, the author reveals and conceals until neither the mystery, nor the suspect can be taken for granted. Chilling ending. —**Bookblog.com Vivian Lake**

On **THE NORTH BEACH MYSTERY SERIES**

[It's] transporting to view San Francisco's colorful Italian-American neighborhood, North Beach, through the eyes of Domenic Stansberry ... really gets under the hood of this part of the city.... in a habit-forming series about Dante Mancuso, a private eye who knows everyone to talk to—or goes to the funeral of anyone unable to talk. —**New York Times Book Review**

"This series... revitalizes the classic detective story, injecting it with a noir sensibility that both evokes the old masters and seems altogether new.—**Booklist** (Starred Review)

Suspense ... Illicit Passion ... Murder ... Stansberry does it with originality, through the freshness of his imagery and the lyricism of his lament for times that change, neighborhoods that grow old and people who can never find their way home. —**New York Times Book Review** *on The Last Days of Il Duce*

Triumphant... a wonderful exercise in lyrical simplicity ... noir in its finest form with near flawless execution and style. -**Baltimore Sun** *on Chasing the Dragon*

Brilliantly imagined ... packs an emotional wallop genre fiction rarely delivers.—**Kirkus** (Starred Review) *on The Ancient Rain*

Takes a seemingly soulless contemporary phenomenon--dot-com speculation--and gives it the same chilling, metaphorical resonance that the postwar noir masters gave to a darkened city street or a tilted Venetian blind. —**BOOKLIST** (Starred Review) *on The Big Boom*

Compelling ... Equal parts contemporary crime fiction and dark, existential poetry.—**Publishers Weekly**

The demographic collision of the area's Italian and Chinese residents serves as an apt metaphor for the cultural (and criminal) forces at play in this complex yet unvarnished story... Stansberry doesn't write with a lot of frills and flourishes. Instead, he stays out of the way of his characters and develops a strong sense of place in which his tale can unfold. —**San Francisco Chronicle on** *Chasing the Dragon*

On **MANIFESTO FOR THE DEAD**

Fascinating, beautifully written—an enviable achievement. **San Francisco Chronicle**

Stansberry's prose is an eerie echo of a dead man's style. And his insights into a writer's anxiety about losing his identity to his characters would make Thompson's own skin crawl.—**New York Times**

Positively hallucinatory.—**LA Weekly**

On **THE SPOILER**

In the tradition of Graham Greene ... a moving chronicle of humanity, disquietingly black and totally absorbing. —**Los Angeles Times**

A sensitive writer and observer... Stansberry knows his baseball and is obviously in love with the game. —**New York Times Book Review**

THE LIZARD

THE LIZARD

DOMENIC STANSBERRY

For Gillian

Molotov Editions

5758 Geary Blvd. #221
San Francisco, C.A. 94121
www.molotoveditions.com

Cover Design: Darcy Fray

Library of Congress Control Number: 2024948950
Hard Bound: 9781948596060 Trade Paper: 9781948596053
First Edition
10 9 8 7 6 5 4 3 2 1

Distributed to the trade by Ingram.

Men will go into caves of the rocks
And into holes of the ground

Isaiah 2:19

PART 1

FUGITIVE

ONE

La Bahia, September

⊏⊐

AFTER THE SHOOTINGS I abandoned my car and wandered in the desert, in cave country, along the fault lines east of Riverside. I was feverish, on the brink of hallucination. An older couple, aging spelunkers, found me and pulled me from the lava tubes. They gave me water and crackers and drove me in their camper as far as the nearest motel cluster. From there I made it west—my head tilted against the Greyhound glass—and eventually up the coast here to La Bahia.

The Hotel La Bahia lies just off the boardwalk, an older building in the Mission style, bleached stucco, with heavy red shutters. It's a squalid place. Sun-baked, poorly ventilated, with tenants who knock up and down the stairs all night.

The heat seems to have followed me from the interior. I lie awake until dawn, until it's cooler inside than out, and I can sleep. Meanwhile, the sun rises. There are no awnings, and the glare beats on the windows until the room heats up all over again. By midafternoon, it is too much. I venture out, squinting toward the ocean. The beach is all but empty, the waves listless. Further down the promenade there are places to sit and drink under a tin roof at the foot of the pier.

Something resembling a breeze drifts from that direction—or is it the illusion of a breeze?—but the last time I went that way I was approached by an activist: an ardent young woman, too ardent, with the face of a seal. She comes every afternoon, carrying her petitions and her pamphlets, to sit at a table under the shade.

I shrug her off the best I can, but for some reason she regards me as sympathetic. My manner, a veneer, remnant of my old life. An open-hearted diffidence belied—as I turn toward the horizon —by my half smile, something darker underneath.

Today, I wander the other direction. I wear my khakis, my shades, a shirt the color of the sand. I am unshaven, a little dirty, but this is not unusual in a beach town. I am all but invisible, I tell myself, though I know it's not true. The streets are emptier in this direction, inland toward the river, but not abandoned. There is movement in the shadows. A man appears behind me, smoking, then vanishes into a motel. A tired-looking woman glints at me from behind the windshield of a parked van. I walk past an enormous man in white shorts into the Café Mosca. A slow, lazy place, ceiling fans overhead and flies pestering the tables. I get a beer and head toward the back. It is an old-style cafe, newspapers scattered about, catering to retirees and the detritus from the beach.

I shuffle through the *Coast Democrat*.

There is no mention of me.

Or the murders in Dulce.

Of course there wouldn't be. It's a local rag and the murders were two states away. There is more online, contradictory stuff—

including pictures that don't much resemble me—but the incident is old news, no longer trending, the kind of brief, violent blossom (a handful dead, others missing, including myself: a former reporter, victim or suspect, not entirely clear) that fades quickly in the face of fresher atrocities. Recent statements, though insisting otherwise, give the impression the authorities have lost interest in my whereabouts.

Logic says they should have located me by now—if indeed they are looking—but between different law enforcement agencies there are gaps in the system, flaws, incompatibilities.

Never mind conflicting priorities.

Human error.

I allow myself a moment's respite, drifting under the soft breeze of the fan, but I don't close my eyes completely. I carry a stiletto in my khakis, in the cargo pocket. I watch the clientele, the in-and-out action at the door—a man who enters suddenly, surveying the counter; a woman fumbling with her purse—but also the ones who linger, drifters and deadbeats. An aging surfer. A Rasta man. A blonde in a stained peasant blouse. On the surface they seem harmless enough, people lost in their own shadows, but it is hard to tell who really is as they seem.

This is the truth:

I miss Renée. I miss my children. I miss my house filled with light and the sounds of traffic rising from Belham Avenue next to the Canal. I miss the coyotes and the smell of wildfire drifting down from the hills. I miss the wrinkled ugliness of my parents, forever vanishing into the dementia of their front porch. I tell myself it wouldn't be so hard to get back, that there is no danger, to myself, to them. I know my way up the coast, over the hills, to the other side of the mountain. Across the gleaming bridge to our little house overlooking the Canal.

Not so far away as the crow flies.

But I am not a crow.

A MAN SHOWS up at the counter, in a yellow golf shirt, a silver earbud nested in his right lobe. Broad shoulders, dark eyes. He gives me a look so empty of expression it is hard to tell whether he is looking at me or through me. Or does he even see me at all? He has black hair and a round face and a cell attached to his belt.

A cop, I think, undercover, but the outfit is too apparent. Security, it occurs to me, of the sort I have seen along the beach. Hired by La Costa Properties, the group that owns the arcade and a good deal of the adjoining property. And lately has struck a community note, working with the cops, social services.

He makes me uncomfortable, and I have learned to follow my instincts. I leave through the back exit down a short hall into a gravel parking lot. There is a cyclone fence, with the river beyond, and a homeless encampment in the trampled lot behind an abandoned motel. A path runs along an embankment above the drainage culvert toward Ocean Avenue.

Outside, the mission bells ring. The tolling echoes down the San Lorenzo River into the Flats, the old Mexican neighborhood that lies in the shadow of the boardwalk. Like Hotel La Bahia, the Flats are slated for destruction. The city intends a convention center. From the embankment, I catch a funeral procession just turning the corner, one such as you might see in a Mexican village—in Jalisco, or Juarez, or East Los Angeles—the peasants carrying a small coffin hung with crepe, the Lady of Guadalupe boosted overhead, a wooden cross held high: a funereal platform burdened up the street under the shadow of the roller coaster on the shoulders of the family, surrounded by relatives and friends, day workers, gangbangers, janitors, alternately solemn, drunk, prayerful, high as kites.

The man in the yellow polo shirt, white as a grub, emerges from La Mosca and stands watching the mourners.

He glances my direction.

I touch the blade in my pocket.

A skink darts from out of the log, across the gravel path. It is long-tailed, with webbed feet, and darts toward the damp grass.

The sun is behind me. My shadow falls long on the street.

It falls longer with every step.

I look back.

The man in the yellow polo shirt has disappeared.

TWO

Earlier

▭

Everyone believes they're born to something special. You must remember that, use it to your advantage. That's what a newspaper editor told me twenty-five years ago, in his office in Sacramento. Idealists are egotists, he insisted; they think their opinions matter—and are likewise virtuous.

"I don't want virtue from you." He eyed me, bemused. Young journalists were notorious for their naivete. Also, their self-importance. "Facts," he said, with a touch of irony. "Nothing but the facts."

He assigned me to crime—shootings, thuggery, gang activity —until I wrote something about corruption on the force. After that, the police no longer talked to me. Then he moved me to the state legislature, a promotion of sorts, but I made the same mistake there. The legislators went mute.

"The truth shall set you free." He spoke fervently, so much so that his mockery became apparent, his underlying cynicism. A professional hazard. He let off. "People talk to the press because they want something. Every once in while you must give it to them."

"It's not my job."

"I'm afraid it is."

I persisted, nonetheless. Soon only the crackpots would talk to me. Mothers of lost causes.

After a while, not even them.

So, I learned what all reporters learn. I could not write a story if no one would speak to me. I also learned there is a gray area that becomes grayer the closer one gets, a place where the fine print becomes too fine to read, and the truth doesn't necessarily exist.

I amended my behavior.

Cultivated, flattered.

Later, our newspaper was sold to Gannett, and I ended up on the other side of the profession, ghosting a weekly column for a state representative. I was good at it and have worked for a lot of people over the years, some well-known: celebrities, politicians, war heroes, people with stories to tell, ambitions, visions to share. I detested them all at times—but I enjoyed it, too, the special treatment, the limousines, the sense of being close to the heart of things, the secret center, an insider, a spinner of the wheel.

None of them regarded me that way.

I was their instrument.

It's the kind of work that wears on you, your head forever bowed to the Dictaphone. It takes its toll. Your skin sloughs off, your tongue grows fat in your mouth. Your identity, if there is such a thing . . .

Well . . .

You glance back at the discarded self, the empty shell, there on the office floor, and wonder just who this new person might be, freshly emerged, wandering down the hall, toes in your shoes.

Breathing though your skin.

Stinking up your shirt.

———

I was at such a point, earlier that last summer—standing outside in the heat, in the backyard weeds—when I received a call from Fred Stinson, a Manhattan literary agent I've worked with off and on. I was home then, in San Rafael. I'd talked to Fred not too long before about a California gubernatorial candidate who wanted a memoir written under his name, something for the national stage—but the candidate had suddenly demurred.

It bothered me . . . a client I'd known a while, a man on the cusp . . . still young but not too young . . . a swarm of light in his blue eyes . . .

It turned out Fred wasn't calling about my politician, but another project, something he thought I might be good for.

"What kind of project?"

"There's confidentially involved," he said. People, when they hire a ghost, have all kinds of privacy concerns. There are non-disclosure papers to sign, sometimes before one even knows the client's name. There are hoops, quizzes, underlings with laptops and recorders, eccentrics who want to get a look at you without being seen, from across a crowded lobby or behind a see-through mirror in an uptown parlor where you sit, legs crossed, inter-viewed by an assistant who suddenly wants to know—after a good deal of aimless banter—your opinion on climate change, on off-shore drilling, on men who have the shape of their noses altered in midlife.

"Well, if you can give me a hint. So I can prepare myself."

"You'll be okay. It's on ground you're familiar with."

"What ground?"

"Max Seeghurs," he said.

I let the name hang there between us, suspended in the cellular ether. I was familiar with Max Seeghurs. More than familiar. Fred knew that. Like me, Max had started out as an investigative reporter in the Central Valley. We'd been close, in a way young men can be close, reckless, competitive, stirring in one another a shared desire for what cannot necessarily be shared. The last time I'd seen Max, it had been maybe a year back, in the humid backwaters of Nebraska, in place called Miscoulga. He'd come with his second wife, Anna, but left for a few days to track down a source in Omaha.

I'd spent some time with her in his absence. They'd been on the verge of splitting, but that split, when it came, I told myself, didn't have much to do with me.

"You and Max, you did some good work together."

"That was a long time ago."

He referred to series of articles we'd done on the drug trade out in the Delta, stories that had gotten some attention but ended in an ugly way when a source we'd been pursuing, a legal intern —young, naïve, doing a stint at Cole & Clark—had been found face down in a ditch the other side of the American River.

It wasn't something I liked to think about.

"You ran into Max last summer, I understand. And his wife, Anna."

I heard something in Fred's voice, maybe, I don't know. I let it pass. Anna was a younger woman. The silence grew, and there was something in the silence, too. I was familiar with these kinds of moments, only from the other side of the table, when I asked a client a question they didn't want to answer. My job in such cases was to know what lay beneath, not so I could reveal it, but so it might be woven with another fabric, and in that weaving become something entirely different.

For Fred, Miscoulga was just passing conversation, talk on the way to somewhere else. The reason he'd called:

"You know that project Max has been working on, *Sundial*. His new book. Regarding that mess down in Santa Fe. He's run into difficulties, sorting that one out."

"That's understandable. It's a tough one."

"You know that world."

"A bit—in passing."

I knew more than that. Several of my clients had made the pilgrimage to the famous Sundial House—my aspiring governor among them, the man on the cusp, with the blue flame in his eyes. People went to mingle with money and celebrity alongside the black-bottomed pool. Licentiousness, drugs. I'd been there myself.

No one went down there anymore.

Sundial's founder was dead: the philanthropist, Mikel Rolland. He'd been found floating in that pool. Ambien in the bloodstream, alcohol. A bump on the head.

An accident . . . officially.

A freak thing . . . an insomniac's blunder . . . overmedicated, wandering from his bedroom for a late-night swim, as he sometimes did, still in his boxers . . . stumbling at the concrete edge ...

His foundation had collapsed shortly after: Sundial, with its new school environmental vision.

"The manuscript could use some help."

"Max and I—"

"I understand Max can be difficult," Fred said. "But you've worked with him, and you've done this kind of work. You know that world. Your name came up."

I'd stepped into projects before, it was true. Not like this one, at least not for some time. But I knew how to wrangle with sensitive material, to cast a glow, or take it away, and how to deal with difficult progenitors.

"You're a good fit," said Fred. "Max thinks so, too."

I wondered about that, but whether Seeghurs welcomed me or not, given the contractual situation, might not much matter. The publisher pulled the trigger. The book was in trouble—otherwise Fred wouldn't be talking to me—and Fred's concern, his business, was to keep things on track.

"It's not just about my commission," he said. "It's reputation. His—and mine. Also, for you . . . there's advantages."

"I'm not a journalist anymore. My clients—"

"Your clients." He pulled up short, treading with caution. "This—it's an opportunity." Fred softened. "That's all. To reinvent yourself, open some new doors. Sometimes, stepping back, into the past, recalibrating oneself, it's a way of moving forward. Last time we talked, you said as much yourself."

I might have said something like that in a winsome moment, inspired by the void in my calendar. Never mind that kind of altruism had been knocked out of me long ago.

I toed the dirt.

"How's the money?" I asked.

Fred told me.

I stepped into the sun. It was hot. No one was home. Renée was at work, the kids out, so it was just me, the dry hills, the birds gliding in the blue air. Fred and I, the silence hung between us, and Max hung in that silence. The money was good, not great. I could walk away, wait things out. Election season was approaching. My blue-eyed client, aspiring governor, shirt sleeves rolled to the elbows—or one of his rivals—I'd worked that world too long to be free of it, those higher ceilings, just out of reach. But I had other considerations. I thought of Miscoulga, of Anna, stepping off the porch away from us both. Of Max Seeghurs, his disheveled look last I'd seen him, the man fraying apart.

Maybe I had stroke of conscience then. Or was it something else? The inexplicable desire to lay oneself bare?

I'd seen it in my clients.

"I'll need the manuscript."

"No."

"No?"

"You know how Max is. He doesn't make anything easy."

"No," I agreed, "he doesn't."

"He wants to talk. In person. You'll have to take the trip out."

That gave me pause. The whole thing did. How much Seeghurs knew, about Anna and me, about my own interactions with Sundial. I had no idea, but Seeghurs could be ruthless. He wasn't going to let go easily. It might have been wiser to stay away. Still, I had people to protect, myself among them.

⬜

THE NEXT DAY I drove to see my parents in Santa Rosa. In the past, these visits had been more festive. Renée would come along, or one of the kids, sometimes the whole group of us, but things had changed. My parents, these last months, seemed to have entered another form of consciousness. They sat for hours in a kind of somnambulist state, eyes lidded, in a wreckage of Solo cups and paper plates.

I'd been slow to acknowledge this transformation until my sister, who'd taken care of them for years, ran off with a bass player from Ukiah, considerably younger.

"I know it's doomed," she told me over the cell, on the way up. "Me and him, that won't last, But I need to have some fun."

"There's nothing wrong with that."

"His last girlfriend pushed him off a cliff."

"Oh. Well."

"It's okay. He bounced," she laughed, joking. It hadn't been a cliff so much as an embankment, behind a karaoke bar, adjoining a gulley of discarded tires. She laughed again, but there was something else there, an irretrievable sadness. "Meanwhile, you and I, we need to make a decision, mom and dad, their living situation. "

"I know."

"Talk to them, please."

Though it was early in the season, there was the smell of smoke in the air, drifting down from a wildfire outside Mendocino. The smoke colored the air. My father was pushing ninety, a decade older than my mother. They'd married late. My father had worked for the government during the latter part of his career, before moving to Santa Rosa, with a pension that had looked pretty good at the time. Now they inhabited that middle zone, not rich, not poor, waiting to go broke before qualifying for assistance. Meantime, we had hired a woman, Mazie, who came by in the evenings. I stopped by every few days to wheel them onto the porch.

My parents liked the sun. They liked the warmth. They kept the house overheated, the thermostat cranked up, no matter the season. It was early June, already warm—but that didn't matter. They brought their sweaters with them onto the porch.

I got there a little before noon.

"I have to leave town for a bit," I said.

It was why I had come, to let them know. My sister wanted me to bring the other matter up. She'd sent me a list of homes.

Valley of the Moon. Golden Hinde.

Grape Mountain.

My mother gave me a sideways glance. She had a blind spot in the center of her vision, macular degeneration, and glimpsed the world in shadows, through the corner of her eyes.

"How long will you be gone?"

"Till the end of the week."

"Vacation?"

"No. It's work."

"Where?"

"Manhattan."

"How lovely." My mother's voice betrayed otherwise. She was blind, arthritic, also envious—and too old to bother to hide it. She missed traveling. "I went there with Betty Thayer, you know." It was a story I'd heard before. "And Margaret Trudeau. Before I met your father."

My father peered up. His eyes were hooded. He moistened his lips and tilted his head toward the sun. Flower-like, reptilian. An old whiptail, taking in the heat. He had his faculties, so far as I could tell, but sometimes slurred his speech.

My mother talked more, but she'd always talked more, and there had always been an element of irreality. She'd spent time at St. Elizabeth's School for Exceptional Young Women, back when the word *exceptional* had somewhat different connotations than now, and mingled with people she might not have known otherwise. She enjoyed talking about them, in intimate ways, including details that might be true or might not. We were alike in that way.

"Even then, she had a thing for older men. Margaret, I mean. And she was promiscuous. So, Pierre was no surprise. Then Fidel . . ." She raised her chin a little. "Their illegitimate son . . . prime minister now." Her gaze fell into the shadows on my left. Lately she'd developed an interest, half-serious, bemused, in an old notion, regaining popularity, that we were ruled by an alien race who wandered among us in human form. "Tabloid nonsense, you might say, but there's a grain there. History tells us. Those people are all related, all the royalty, so-called. They sleep with whoever they please. Cousins. Commoners. Goats."

"Sheep," my father corrected. He'd spent time in the English countryside. "More docile, domestic."

"See that . . ." my mother said.

"Goats are problematic. The noises they make. Also, those horns."

"See that," she said again. "Your father, he's still sharp. Both of us. I know your sister's been talking to you. But see, our conversation. Animal husbandry. World affairs. We have our senses."

"Mostly," my father said.

"Eighty-nine per cent," said my mother. "Good for our age."

"Also, our looks."

"We are not ugly."

My mother had dark skin, deeply lined, and thick silver hair. She was Castilian, a descendant of Spanish royalty, or so she claimed, refugees from Franco's Civil War. My father had no such pedigree. He'd been raised in foster homes. He'd done a stint in the Navy and gone on to be a communications engineer, working on advanced telemetries and missile tracking systems for the Defense Department. Part of his work had involved traveling abroad, silo to silo, all over Europe. He had a high security clearance, and there'd been some glamour, a trip to Cannes with a French ambassador, now dead, who'd had an affair with Gina Lollobrigida.

It had been a badge of honor, that security clearance, though a problem as well—the paranoia. Unexpected visitors, questioning this, that.

I knew the feeling. Ever since I could remember.

That of someone watching.

"So—can you tell us?"

"What?"

"Who you working for?"

"Not yet. It's all preliminary, and confidential. If we go forward, maybe later."

"You always say that, but we never hear. Meanwhile, your own life, your real life . . . how things are at home, Renée, the children. You keep that quiet, too."

"Life is good," I said.

She reached toward the sound of my voice, feeling my face: my brow, my nose, running her fingers over my lips, the bump in my chin. "People say you resemble me." She preened a little. My hair was black, like hers, but also curly, cropped short. Jewish blood, a family rumor, centuries back. Forced conversion during the Inquisition. (A tenuous claim, gleaned by mother's maiden aunt from the registries in Andalusia, dating back past the Church, the Moors, the Romans, to the scrawlings on ancient caves.) "But underneath you're more like your father," my mother said. "Everything, you keep it all locked up. I understand. We all have a life inside we can't talk about."

The angle of the light changed on the porch, slanting hard and low over the eaves. My mother's brow beaded with sweat. I wiped her face, and my father's too, then wheeled them inside. I needed to be home before too late, and Mazie would be by soon.

"I'd like some fried chicken," my father said.

"Next time, Dad."

"You always say that."

"I promise."

My father had trouble with the bones. The doctor had said to avoid it, but there was a place in Cotati—next to the Miwok Casino—and I knew how much my father loved that chicken. "I promise," I said again. Then I rolled them in front of the television. They wanted their blankets, their sweaters. It was hotter inside than out, but I brought them anyway. I gave them each a kiss on the cheek. Then I slid open the slider, to let in some air through the screen.

"No," my mother said. "Shut it, please."

I found Renée sitting on the edge of the infinity pool, her dress hiked up, feet dangling in the water. Our yard was terraced into a rise at the end of the street, the dry hills above us and the bluff below, alongside a sudden canyon, a dry wash snaking down a concrete gulley into the Canal District.

I sat next to Renée, on the edge of the pool, too, but facing her, my back to the water. The light was all but gone from the sky.

"When are you leaving?"

It was simple question that seemed freighted.

"Tomorrow."

I couldn't read her. I didn't know if she wanted me to come or go. Renée sipped her drink. She had beautiful lips. She'd been born in St. Louis, but her mother, who'd been raised in Paris, couldn't stand it there. Renée had been a language student when I met her—an intern at the legislature who wanted to go into diplomatic service.

"You could come with me."

"I have my own work."

"You could take some time off."

"There's the kids."

The kids were old enough to take care of themselves. They weren't wild or untrustworthy. Rather, they tended to get preoccupied, to lose sense of time. To forget about the faucet filling the bathroom tub until the next morning when the hall carpet was the texture of moss and water trickled down the stairs.

"When I get back, we can go someplace together, just the two of us."

"I remember Max Seeghurs," she said. "I met him that once,

when you were still at the paper. A good-looking man. Talented."

"Yes."

"He has a difficult reputation?"

I shrugged.

"Everyone has a difficult reputation."

"Has Gaddis called?"

Gaddis was the politician who'd shied away from the memoir, our current lieutenant governor, running for governor, but with ambitions beyond that. Jim Gaddis, my man on the cusp. A riser. I'd invested time in him, close up. Studied the video clips: the easy smile, hair swept back, just a touch of gray. I'd helped him with some scandal triage a while back—and gone jogging with him a few times since. So I knew his personal story, his strengths, his weaknesses, his blue eyes, but maybe that was the problem. His press secretary had stopped returning my calls.

"We're still talking. Fred's optimistic," I said.

I took her by the ankle. The moon was low on the horizon, a fat moon, creeping up as the color fell out of the sky. Something moved in the brush, on the other side of the hog wire. A coyote, maybe. A neighborhood cat. There were kids out there too, creeping about, as were the homeless who wandered the path up from Trader Joe's in the shopping center at the base of the cliff. There was the barrio below us, and the wealthier homes above. The hills stretched for a long way, all the way to the ocean, and the darkness rolled in from that direction, over those hills. All of a sudden, I didn't want to leave.

"What about Miscoulga? Are you going back there this summer?"

Miscoulga was a retreat in the Midwest. It wasn't as well-known as some of the other retreats, legendary for the debauched smell of their bedsheets. It wasn't the type of place I'd seek out of my own accord. I'd gone on account of a client who'd paid me to

occupy the cottage next to him—to help with an autobiograph-
ical article about his deep roots in a midsize Midwestern town
served by the small airline where he was the chief executive.
Only he'd been called away after a few days, leaving me there to
finish the piece.

"To Miscoulga? No, not this summer," I said. "There's no
reason."

"No?"

"He's moved to Los Angeles. New position, new company,
with their own public relations."

This happened. Clients talked for hours, revealing themselves—creating a vision, an identity—but then things shifted. A
new vision was needed, a new ghost. Meanwhile, the darkness
was all but complete. I could see a small light bobbing on the hill,
a hiker working down the path that dropped through the oaks
and emerged on the other side of that gulley. Renée pulled her
feet from the water.

"Do you ever want to live a different kind of life?"

Her question surprised me.

"No, not me. I love this life."

"Me too."

She shivered and kissed me. It was a hungry kiss. She pushed
her tongue into my mouth and I put my hand on the hem of her
dress, fisting the material. I remembered the damp mud in
Miscoulga, how it felt between my fingers as I leaned back, both
hands splayed, and Anna Seeghurs looming over me in the grass.
I reached up between my wife's legs and touched that soft trian-
gle, looking into her eyes, and remembered the mosquitos
ponding on my neck, the sweat pooling under my arms in the
Nebraska humidity, the buzz of the cicadas, and the monks who
cloistered in the monastery above the Miscoulga retreat. Anna
and I had run into them the next morning on the path, freshly
washed but still smelling of sex. A light went on in the house, our

daughter's room. Her head appeared briefly at the window. A car pulled up into the wash at the end of our street. It sat there a while.

"We should go inside."

"No."

We took off our clothes and went into the infinity pool. How the water fell off its edge gave the illusion of the sea merging with the sky. The sensation was of floating in ether, as if your body were not your own but inhabited by someone far away. When we touched each other, it had a soft, delicious quality, not quite real. Then we were ourselves again, shivering as we climbed from the pool.

The kids had abandoned the television downstairs. Their voices sounded as if they came from elsewhere. I didn't recognize the show, but it was familiar nonetheless, the insistent muttering. I'd had a similar feeling back in Santa Rosa at my parents' house. It was somehow as if the spaces were connected—all spaces, here, now—but me, myself, this skin in which I moved, was no longer my own, and I was filled with trepidation.

The same trepidation that I feel now, here in La Bahia, wandering the too bright streets—wanting nothing more than to shed that feeling, to crawl out of this lost world and back into my beautiful life.

THREE

▭

I BOUGHT A pack of cigarettes and lit up on the corner. I did not smoke at home, but it was the first thing I did when I went on a trip. I paused on 42nd Street looking down the maw toward Broadway. It was a nasty taste, insubstantial, poisonous, but I liked the rawness in my chest.

My cell rang. Entranced by the glittering boards around me, the flashing pulse, distracted, I inhaled as I answered.

"You're smoking," Renée said.

"No."

A subway shed stood across the street: the old Q line, out to Queens, where Anna Seeghurs lived since the break-up. I'd been out there a couple times—reckless, on thin ice—but that was over.

"Just getting some air."

"What kind of air?"

"All your French friends are smokers," I said. It was a fact. I smelled it on her when she came from her appointments at the embassy. Sometimes those appointments ran late.

"Not all of them."

"Roosevelt, too. He loved to smoke."

It was my job to study politicians, propaganda, what stuck in the public mind, what didn't. Photographs of Roosevelt showed him with the cigarette holder, debonair, sophisticated, though in reality he smoked fiendishly—in his wheelchair—unfiltered butt between his fingers, scattering ash all over his slacks. Overhead, the corner Jumbotron fell from color to black and white, sepia tone, a hopeless nostalgia, the city dwelling in its past: parades and ticker tape from days gone by, astronauts, baseball players, politicians, an open top limo, a woman happy, elated, embracing a soldier returned from war.

"So did Kennedy. Those small cigars."

"He's dead."

"And Obama."

She sighed. Something in that sigh—the slowness of it, how she luxuriated in her exasperation—made me wonder if she were smoking herself. But she was right about the presidents. They were no kind of role model. Obama had started out vigorous enough, like all of them, but he looked sickly by the end, thin, jaundiced. His people tried to hide that. Photoshopped the hell out of him. Put him on jet skis, Michele waving from the shore.

I almost preferred the new man, the demon in the orange hair. The Antichrist, whatever his name.

I snubbed the butt out on the walk.

"Where are you?"

"Home."

"The kids?"

"Lena's busy with her butterfly collection."

It was unusual for a girl my daughter's age to be obsessed with insects. I didn't know whether to be proud or worried. Our son, despite his forgetfulness, was less of a concern. A straightforward mammalian creature who liked to chase the ball around the yard.

"Before I forget, your mother called."

"The landline?"

"She gets the numbers mixed. A couple of men stopped by—to talk to your father. It worried her."

My mother couldn't see well, and she had suspicions, not completely unwarranted. When he'd been with the Defense Department, my father would get visits, debriefings around security matters. These had continued a while after he retired. There'd been ongoing security issues, regarding the Turks, the Israelis. Such visits were rare now. My mother—given her eyesight, her hearing (failing, too) and habits of thought—had a way of misperceiving. Or seeing behind the veil, depending.

"Mazie's husband, he helps out sometimes. Along with her son. It might have been them."

"She says they were asking questions about you."

"She gets confused," I said, though it made me wonder. I'd been checked out myself by overzealous clients. "I'll call her."

Renée was a good-looking woman, intelligent, fluent in several languages. French, German, Spanish. Even a little Arabic and Japanese. It was part of the thing that had attracted me to her, I guess, the fact I could not quite figure who she was. A good part of the work she'd been doing lately was through referral by a friend at one of the embassies in the city, an older man she'd known since college. She was a little taller than me, a little older, but she didn't seem to age, not really—and moved in a realm just beyond my ability to possess her.

"I have to go into the city tomorrow evening," she said.

"Why?"

"The French," she said. "Clients who want entertaining."

"La Rouche?"

"At the consulate."

The consulate held cultural events, mixers for French business—also individual scientists, artists, technologists—seeking to deepen local affiliations. La Rouche was an old firm, known for its cultural face, its charming emissaries. Too charming, some of them.

"They'll be others there."

She didn't say anything more about this and neither did I. Those clients, those French, she kept the particulars to herself, and I did not seek to retrieve them. We had an agreement, unspoken. (Or maybe it was just me, a deal I'd made with myself.)

The duplicity was all within.

A man wandering by asked for a cigarette. I obliged him. I passed the subway entrance, glanced down the rumbling stairs, the dirty concrete, the passage to Queens, out to Anna's. I wavered. There comes a time when you question your motivations: the idiot compulsion to repeat the past, to seek out your own undoing. I'd seen it in my clients, how, despite the carefully crafted stories, they betrayed themselves, trundling their guilt into the light. I turned from the subway and headed out of the square under a scaffold along the street. Back at the hotel I called Santa Rosa and let it ring. No one answered. This wasn't surprising, no reason to worry. The cell, even if they were awake—even if the ringer was on—might be difficult to find in the dark.

PART 2

THE DANGLING MAN

FOUR

New York City

THE NEXT DAY I went to meet with Fred Stinson, of Stinson &
Hill. It was an old agency, a small one—with a dying cachet, to
be honest—founded by Emily Hill, one of the first woman agents
in the business. She was stepdaughter to one of the Rothschilds,
and had slept with the Fitzgeralds, both of them, if the rumors
were true. Either way, the rumors had been good for business
back when people still cared about the Fitzgeralds. Emily had
taken Fred as a partner several decades back. She had passed, so
it was just Fred now, with an assistant he made occasional refer-
ence to. Fred was close to sixty, some dozen years older than me.
He wore a suit jacket over a T-shirt, a good-looking man with
thick gray hair and high cheekbones.

We met in Chelsea near the old hotel, famous during its long
decline for its degenerate clientele—artists, junkies, transients—a
mix of losers and celebrities, impoverished nobodies, highbrows

on the slum, all side-eyeing each other in the glamorous, dirty, fucked-up hallways.

There is a bar around the corner where they all used to go in the day: a dark-paneled place with a musty décor. In the far back, a door opened onto an alley with some tables and chairs, an iron-fenced patio where—by virtue of some loophole in city ordinance—the customers could smoke and vape.

"There are rules," Fred winked. "And then there are rules."

Something about Fred: he could make you feel special—in the manner the newspaperman had insisted—as if you were born to something. "And so," he said. "How are things going with you out there?"

"They're fine."

He raised his eyebrows, and I could tell he knew otherwise. Maybe it was my manner, or word just got around. Truth was, though I didn't much admit it, I'd been having trouble nailing things down. New clients flirted but didn't bite, and the old ones had begun to drift.

"They'll come back to you," Fred said. "Not everyone can do what you do."

"I know."

"Fuck 'em if they don't."

"Yes."

"You've reinvented yourself before."

The tendency these days was toward true believers. A good ghost probed the weaknesses in his clients' stories and challenged the details to make the story stronger. But that brand of professionalism was out of fashion. Clients wanted conviction, passion, unfettered belief. The longer you'd been around, the more suspect you were, until eventually you were just obsolete. Fred, on the other hand, was an old-school guy, the kind who bought you drinks and food and smoked incessantly and liked to linger at the table, who charmed you half to death by telling you how brilliant you were, how everything was about to break your way. I liked this. I enjoyed the treatment. Fred carried his cigarettes in a leather case, and I liked that, too. He shook one out for me, and I leaned back, taking in the moment.

The waitress came by with a cocktail menu listing specialty drinks named after diplomats and politicians from the Cold War. The place catered to an older crowd, all but extinct, who enjoyed mulling around in their extinction. The waitress seemed disappointed when I ignored the menu and ordered a bourbon from the well.

"Things have changed," Fred said, a refrain of his, usually about the business, some sorry piece of news.

"The publisher . . .?"

"No, this regards Max."

"What's the issue?"

"He won't return my calls."

Max's reputation was not undeserved. He was difficult, just for the hell of it, but it was also endemic to the way he worked. He went in deep on the investigative end, sometimes under false identity. The strategy put him at risk, not just with those he investigated—politicians with underworld connections (unproven), financiers, cops—but with the intelligence community itself. The Feds harangued him. He was on a government watch list because of an affair he'd had with the mistress of an Israeli arms dealer. A senator from Kansas —whose family sold hogs to China—had slapped him with a libel suit over kickback allegations.

Meanwhile, Max's personal life had fallen into shambles. Obsessed with work, hounded by creditors, twice divorced. His own fault, one could argue: the constant affairs—with women he'd met in the field, sources, assistants, just about anyone.

"I'm concerned," said Fred.

"Me, too." I said, though I'd never expected Max at this meeting. He'd make me go to him.

———

It wasn't just Max. The people I worked for, they all led double lives.

I knew all about it.

The need for attention, glamour.

Or just to escape.

Human enough.

In Miscoulga, my client, an airline executive—a sincere man, regular sort, humble roots (that was the pitch, anyway, the smell of broomcorn, washed plaid)—had been called away suddenly, a new opportunity ahead, and I watched his humility vanish down the steps. I might have left then, but Max had shown up at the colony a few days before, together with Anna. He'd come to work, to drink, and she'd come with him, but things between them were pretty much finished. She still loved him, she told me later— women always loved Max—but she wanted out of his shadow.

She had her own ambitions.

Not long after arriving, Max had headed alone up to Omaha. He went to track down a source, his return delayed, as it was often delayed. He didn't call, as of course he wouldn't—the reception was lousy anyway—and Anna and I spent some time talking on the big porch at the main house.

The next day, we went out to a pond, a place fed by an underground spring, an upwelling from the Platte River that had been a place of some significance to the Pawnee.

Anna had gray eyes, the color of that water, and a big shock of black hair, unruly, the kind of wild hair, just looking, I felt the desire to clutch in my fists both at once. She pulled that hair back off her neck, there in the heat, and something about that gesture, the cast of her eyes, the turn of her cheek, belied her ambition and vulnerability: the sense of idealism, already betrayed, forever lost.

Or maybe that was all in me.

The smell of her, a younger woman, East Coast college, money, the legislative halls she'd started roaming lately, her new job, lobbying for a nonprofit.

She regarded me, studying my face, my profile. My Sephardic nose (so labeled by my mother's maiden aunt, who— never mind our Jewish roots (alleged)—slept every night with a crucifix over her bed). I'd told Anna something of my life, bits and pieces—stories about Renée, the people I worked with. She was drawn to that. Or what she imagined it to be.

"A place like this . . . One must watch oneself," she said.

"Why?"

"You know what I mean. The world out there, it's far away. We might feel like it doesn't exist. It's just us."

She faltered, shy, then reached out to touch my face. I lost my hand in her hair.

It was a sweet moment, almost. It felt innocent, as betrayal often does.

An old story, nothing new about it.

The kind of thing . . . easy to tell yourself later it didn't matter, just something that happened far from home.

The truth, as always, was elsewhere.

▭

"Seeghurs has gone off track," Fred said. "He's lost focus—he meanders."

"He always meanders," I said. "His meandering, I thought that was a selling point."

"Not this time."

Max Seeghurs had his blind spots, like every reporter: Hunches based on obsessions, preconceptions, that did not always prove true.

He got tangled sometimes, chased the wrong things.

"He's lost the thread."

To be fair, the circumstances surrounding Mikel Rolland's death and the collapse of Sundial invited confusion. Heir to an industrial fortune, an eccentric with an almost mystic attachment to the Southwest, Mikel Rolland had dismantled the family empire to start Sundial: an environmental foundation based on the Circulist model, seeking reintegration of desiccated lands into the human sphere.

The goal was to transform industrial wastelands, ruined waterfronts, strip-mined mountains. Ambitions projects that defied easy classification.

And triggered their share of greed and disarray.

"The original idea," Fred said, "was to explore this maverick philanthropist, Mikel Rolland, and his legacy—a flawed legacy, to be sure, but well intended. A very American story, really. Every bit as ambitious as his forefathers. But Rolland was seduced. He liked parties, he liked celebrity." Fred paused, looking at me in a profound way, then shook his head. "The man had blind spots. Certain people may have used that to advance their own interests. Certainly, after his wife passed—he left himself vulnerable."

Mikel Rolland's generosity, his money, had drawn attention, not just of the like-minded but of the usual suspects—and the tabloids. Glamour and wealth mixed with tragedy. His wife, taken by leukemia. Their adopted son, in and out of trouble. A reckless kid, dead now too, within months of his father.

The foundation had collapsed soon after.

All this inspired endless speculation, based on the notion, persistent but unsubstantiated, that Sundial had been infiltrated over the years, its various projects used in systematic fashion as fronts for laundered money, origins in illegal trafficking.

Money that worked its way back into legitimate business, all but impossible to trace, immune from investigation.

With the Feds in on the game.

"That speculation, that noise, it's part of the story, yes. But I'm afraid Max has gone off on a tangent, resurrecting old conspiracy theories. Sometimes the truth is what you see. A man goes out for a late-night swim. He's had a bit too much to drink. He hits his head, and he dies. Then the world he created, it falls apart."

"What about the son?"

Fred shrugged. "The kid had issues . . ."

The son's death had been sudden, violent—a knife in the gut, back alley, while soliciting sexual favors in Santo Domingo. According to the Dominican police, at least. Not everyone believed it. Just as they didn't believe the Justice Department's assessment that nothing in Sundial's divestiture merited investigation. Max Seeghurs, of course, would be skeptical. It was a journalist's job. Also, he had his own issues with Justice.

I understood that, but I also understood what Fred was getting at. The speculation, the noise—the endless conspiracy chatter, especially the wild stuff—shape shifters . . . illuminati ... alien agents in cahoots with the CIA. This obscured the real story.

"There's no there there," said Fred. "Nothing tangible."

My guess: accuracy was not the publisher's primary concern. Factual nonsense, conspiracy accusations, these were bread and butter, but there were lines to navigate. The earlier lawsuit had been enjoined, and lawyers were hovering. The publisher did not want more libel. Or problems with the Senate Intel Committee.

My job would be to wash the thing.

"I'll need the manuscript," I said.

Fred beckoned the busboy. The wait staff seemed to have vanished, and he wanted another drink.

"That's the problem."

"What?"

"Seeghurs, the eccentric. No cell, no computer. He has this notion he's being followed. You can't go anywhere with him. He's moved out of his old office, into some dive studio out in Coney Island. He keeps his manuscript in the freezer compartment in his refrigerator, for Chrissake."

This peculiarity was not Seeghurs' invention but inherited from an earlier generation who had worked on paper and used the refrigerator freezer as a household fire safe, never mind its questionable utility as such.

"Have you read it?"

"Part," Fred said. "An early draft—hard copy. He left it a few days, then came back, impatient for a reaction." He shrugged. "He didn't like what I had to say. Evocative, brilliant. In places. I told him that. But just fucking muddled. Unsupported speculation. I told him that, too. He didn't like hearing it. He took his draft and stomped off. But he didn't argue. He knows it's a mess."

"Did he say that?"

"He's got a source, he claims, on the verge."

Seeghurs enjoyed working on the margins, the edge of chaos, pursuing angles others let lie. His habit, when a story didn't gel, he'd claim a source in the wings.

Sometimes it was true.

"The key, he says, a missing piece."

"If he won't return your calls, why would he return mine?"

"You've worked together. Also, Sundial, you know the lay of the land, the players. You can help."

"If he's not picking up . . ."

"Go out to Coney Island and knock on his door."

In the old days, that task, chasing him down, had fallen my way more than once. I wondered if Seeghurs was even out in Coney Island. I'd seen this before. He'd go solo, rogue, deadline looming, then come back last minute, that sloppy brilliance all over the page, observation mixed with the unverifiable. Fact that needed to be checked, then checked again.

That task had fallen my way as well.

"There's also his wife, Anna," Fred said.

"I thought they were split."

"They're still close. She worked with him, helped with research. Typed up his notes, his manuscripts. She may have copies. Or know where he is. I tried talking to her, but she snowballed me. So, I was thinking, as an old friend, a colleague, you might have better luck."

I wasn't so sure. The break between Anna and me had been clean, mutual—a private matter, ended as swiftly as it had begun, discreetly, before any palpable disaster—but everything left its trace.

"She's over in Queens," said Fred.

I already knew that but held my tongue.

A waitress came to the table. It was a different waitress than before. She brought the same list of Cold War cocktails, but it was happy hour now, and everything was cheaper.

Fred offered me another cigarette.

I shook my head no, then took it anyway.

I considered the menu. The Churchill over ice. A Marilyn Manhattan. An Ernest Hemingway, neat, in a double-barrel glass. Fred tilted forward with his lighter.

"What will it be?" asked the waitress.

I nodded to Fred.

He lit my cigarette.

I ordered a Third Man, named for the old movie—rye, absinthe, a touch of bitters—and leaned back to smoke.

FIVE

In most jurisdictions there is no legal requirement to report a body to the police. It may not be wise—depending on one's relation to the dead—but it is not against the law to ignore a corpse. I'd learned this while working for *The Register*, covering a story about a meth addict living in a trailer, out in the delta, in tule country, whose young wife had died of an overdose. The man had still been living there, his trailer floor littered with ice cream cartons, potato chip bags, syringes, when the cops came to investigate the stench. The police couldn't charge the man with murder, because he hadn't administered the dose—and there was, despite the public outcry, no crime in living in squalor, with a corpse or without.

This incident occurred to me the next day, on the subway out to Coney Island, a long ride, down into the underground: a quick gray view when the train rose out of the tunnel before pummeling back under Brooklyn, under Flatbush and Gravesend all the way to Coney Island. The journey brought to mind my time as a reporter, assigned the hopeless cases, the ones you learned to realize—with morbid premonition—would end in some ugly, tangled place.

With the addict living in a trailer, the path had led further out into the tules, to a plethora of meth labs on property owned by an offshore LLC, a shell company within a shell, administered by a signature on a piece of paper—whose real owner lay somewhere beneath an impenetrable legal surface.

This was where Seeghurs had come in, because a young woman, a law student interning at Cole and Clark, had flirted with him at a bar on J Street. The next morning, while slipping on her stockings, she'd mentioned her firm's involvement in the creation of such shells.

"She can do some digging," Seeghurs told me.

"Fine," I said. "But let me talk to her. It's my story."

He shook his head.

"She's my source."

I'd sought her out anyway, an ambitious young woman with pale eyes who let me take her for a drink. She turned reticent, but later, outside her door, pressed her check against mine. Whispered two words:

Money laundering.

Which didn't tell me much, since everybody knew how drug money moved through the offshore shells. I pursued her for a while, though I don't know if it was because of the feel of her cheek against my own, or because what I feared she might be telling Seeghurs that she wasn't telling me.

A couple weeks later, the cops pulled her from the mud under the docks.

Max and I blamed ourselves, each other, the dead woman herself. She'd paid a visit to the DA's, to Justice, the local office— according to an anonymous phone call, a timorous voice—though Justice itself had no comment. The police released their report.

Homicide, probable.

Death by blunt trauma. Tire iron to the head.

No suspect, no motive.

That's the way it was, sometimes. You got the brute facts but still didn't know what had happened.

There is a river walk there now. Hotels . . . high-end stuff . . . bistros and shops frequented by lobbyists and political types. I'd been to fundraisers for Gaddis, my aspiring governor, at a luxury condo overlooking the spot where she'd been found. I remember Jim Gaddis out there on the balcony, facing the river, in his white shirt, sleeves rolled up, assessing the future.

He'd been instrumental in getting that project off the ground. It had been seeded by Sundial.

The train reached the end of the line at the Stillwell Station. Max lived a good way past the subway terminus, a long walk, some twenty blocks down Neptune Avenue. The avenue had been hit by the hurricane a few years back—but there were still boarded-up groceries, lots full of debris, forsaken high-rises ruined on the lower floors by sewage from the surge. I walked down Neptune—past the squat brownstones and the still squalling amusement center—all the way to Seagate, a gated neighborhood fronted by the Atlantic on one side but otherwise surrounded by public housing. Back in the day, uptown money and mobsters colonized Seagate. Mostly now, who one saw on the street anyway, it was Russians and Poles, also Hasidic Jews in their black hats and their beards. I had to walk through the gate to get in, past a security guard in a booth.

"Maxwell Seeghurs," I said.

The gatekeeper regarded me blithely.

"You're not him."

"No, I'm here as a visitor. I came to see Max."

I told him my name, the one I used for projects such as this, working as a ghost. He asked me to repeat it.

"S.E. Reynolds."

"Your name, not your initials."

I had been through this before. My name was my initials. To clarify things, I handed him a business card. He wanted to see the driver's license as well. This was going to cause confusion. Usually, this kind of visit, it wasn't a problem, but I hadn't anticipated the security check.

"These names are not the same."

I explained it to him. For professional purposes, I worked under different names. There was my professional name, S. E. Reynolds, under which most people knew me—and there was my real name, the legal one, that I used for everything else.

"You have two names?"

I nodded.

"Like Lady Gaga."

"Yes," I said. "Like Lady Gaga."

"And Ice-T."

"Him, too. And Huey Long."

"The cartoon duck?"

"Yes, the cartoon duck. He ran for president."

He snorted. I snorted, too. He looked down at the visitor log, pen in hand, as if deciding which of my alleged names to write. He returned to the question of the initials. It amused him.

"They must stand for something."

I didn't answer.

"S as in Steve?"

"If that works for you."

"Or is it Sallie?"

He laughed, a Cossack-sounding laugh, as if he wouldn't mind sticking his pen into my throat. We'd been talking about different Hueys, after all, different ducks. He picked up the guardhouse phone, and I figured he was calling Max, which might end the whole business right there (no telling how Seeghurs might react), but whoever was on the other end, the guard spoke to him in Russian. I heard my two names mixed in there with all the Slavic talk, and Seeghurs' name, too. When the conversation ended, the guard gave me a desultory nod.

"He's there?"

"Who?"

"Seeghurs?"

"I don't know."

"Who were you talking to?"

"What does it matter? You have the house number. Go in, you want to go in. Up to you."

Seagate may have been a private community, gated away, sheltered from the knife boys, the carnies and the gimcrack girls, aging whores, mermaids in their spangled lingerie—but here, close to the cyclone fence, it had a battered look. Partly this was on account of the hurricane. The storm had left its mark. The police department hadn't been rebuilt and stood on blocks, housed in aluminum trailers. Some big houses stood untouched, also some more modest places—the kind where several genera- tions lived under one roof—and a row of dismal brownstones. The surge had been uneven. Here and there, lots were scraped clean, houses boarded up, red tags nailed to the door. The lane curled back on itself, down toward where the seawall had broken.

There was light everywhere, but it wasn't what one might call a friendly light. It was the hard light from the gray Atlantic. Seeghurs' place hunched a block from the beach, a tiny stand- alone, narrow setbacks on either side, a small apartment over a padlocked garage. How the wave had broken, the building survived. The block had a gap-toothed look. Closer to the water, a large house sagged at the middle, surrounded by chain link. I stood on Seeghurs' porch, on the decaying slats, and saw the eviction notice tacked to the door behind the frayed screen.

No one responded to my knock. I peered through the smudged window: a small kitchen where the table served as a desk, an old Royal on top, a ream of yellow paper of the type once found in newspaper offices. An interior door opened to another room, a glimpse of the ocean beyond. I knocked again. I was probing the window casing—to see if it might slide open—when a man appeared on the walkway, a thick-shouldered man in an open-collared shirt.

"What are you doing?"

"I'm looking for Max Seeghurs."

"You a friend of his?"

The man spoke with a Russian accent. I gathered he was not particularly fond of Seeghurs, and likewise suspicious of me.

"It's business."

"That's not what you tell Vosh."

"Vosh?"

"Voshki. My man at the gate."

"He misunderstood."

"So, what are you, if not friend? Bill collector?"

"A colleague."

He nodded, a desultory nod, like Voshki at the gatehouse. "I rent him the place against my better judgment—him and his girlfriend."

"Girlfriend?"

"He paid six months in advance. Cash. But now it is month seven, going on eight. And well, I am holding the bag."

"That's not good."

"No."

"It's a shame."

"It is fucking shame."

"I'm sorry."

I had no reason to apologize. It was a habit, even for transgressions that had nothing to do with me. The man seemed to accept this, nodding as if, of course, I was to blame. Himself, meanwhile, he was not inclined to forgive.

"I lose rent, that's what it means. I know routine. I put note on door—note disappear . . . So, I put another note . . . Meanwhile your buddy, your colleague, he disappear. Last minute, I am afraid, he will show up at housing court—'I never get note, house unsafe, landlord won't fix, rat hole with no heat.' The usual lies."

"The woman, what was her name?"

"Which one?"

"What do you mean?"

"Yah, hah," he laughed. "There were two. One who helps him move in. Around sometimes. And the other one, show up sudden. Around few weeks. Very low profile. Sleeps on cot." He laughed again. "I don't know. Not my business."

"Black hair?"

"What?"

"The first woman? Thick? Out like this?" I gestured as if something wild were growing out of the top of my head.

He looked at me skeptically.

"What is it you want, anyway?"

I'd felt such skepticism often enough when I was a reporter. Fallback behavior, I'd learned back then, when someone asked a question I didn't want to answer, I'd pretend I hadn't heard—and ask another one back. It wasn't the most brilliant strategy, but it worked more often than you might think.

"You have a lease agreement? Names—emergency contacts?"

"Of course, of course. Everything on file." He made a dismissive motion, and with that little wave of the hand, I knew he had nothing. He pointed at himself then, tapped his chest. "Mind like steel trap. Never forget a name." As if to prove himself, he recited my name back to me, then pointed at nearby houses, naming the residents. "Even your Mr. Seeghurs, and that first woman, Mrs. Black Hair, I meet her only once. And that other female . . ." He paused then, looking away, and I saw the name of the latter, whoever it was, had gotten lost in that steel trap.

His phone saved him.

"I have appointment," he said. "Tenant, trouble with her appliances. I tell her, don't worry, I am a timely man, available at your convenience.'" He laughed. "So, here she is, vibrating in my pocket."

He checked his phone, smiling with unabashed, lascivious pleasure. "But let me tell you, every time you rent to somebody, it's a chance. References, credit, lease, internet report—all that means nothing. Cash more important. Place like this, here on beach, I put rent sign in window, gone in minute . . . I don't have time for the computer. I should know better, I know."

"He paid you cash?"

"Yes, that was factor, too."

"Can I look around?"

"Eviction—is not an easy matter. I can't touch his things. Squatter's rights."

He toyed with his phone screen. Thumbed a response. "Widow Klinski. She likes to make you wait. Her—in her beautiful yellow convertible." He tapped his toe. We'd reached a stalemate. I repeated my question: "Can I look around?"

"You want to rent the place?"

"It wasn't in my thoughts."

"Against the law, for me to enter the tenant's dwelling unless I have some legitimate business in there."

"It's legitimate if I want to rent the place?"

"Your friend, he want you to pick up his lease, short term, long term, something like that, maybe, okay. If you make agreement with him, shared space, he travels a lot, whatever . . . but I need a small deposit. Application fee."

"How much?"

"Sixty bucks."

I thumbed out a pair of twenties but not the third. I thumbed them without speaking. He didn't like it, maybe, but neither did I, and he took the money, stoic, without complaint.

"Non-refundable."

What I'd seen from the window was pretty much it, just the kitchen and a small room behind. The place was nothing special, but it didn't look recently abandoned: a made bed, clean dishes in the kitchen rack, the work desk orderly. A little too orderly for someone in the middle of a project, especially Seeghurs. No manuscript boxes, no binders, no folders of loose, untethered pages. Also, none of those countless notebooks in which he scribbled incessantly. Dust layered the top shelf unevenly, absent in places, suggesting objects had been moved, displaced.

"Nice little kitchen, with workspace. And ocean view, here, from bedroom slider." The Russian played it out, as if I might rent the place. "Nice mattress, comfortable chair. Furniture all comes with apartment. Including cot—for visitors," he smiled. "Also dishes. Refrigerator."

I caught an unpleasant smell, mold, maybe, rot, stronger in the bedroom, as if an animal had died in the wall. I examined the closet space. Seeghurs' clothes. Dress shirts and pants. A nice sport coat. T-shirts and sweaters folded onto an interior shelf, a pair of expensive shoes. Stuff he might want, but nothing he'd miss terribly.

A suitcase stood on the other side of the bed. "More storage underneath."

"In the garage?"

"Not garage anymore. Sealed off. You enter from back." He gestured at the landing, at the stairs headed down.

I nodded at the suitcase.

"Was that here before?"

"I don't know."

Its presence, together with the items left behind, left the situation open to interpretation. The cot, a simple affair, folded nearby, suggested something other than romance.

The Russian opened the slider—to help air the place, I supposed—and gazed toward the ocean.

"Good salt air."

"Yes," I said.

"We don't have much crime here."

"No?"

I opened the refrigerator in the manner of a prospective tenant—remembering that Seeghurs sometimes used the freezer as a manuscript safe. But I saw no manuscript, just some frozen egg rolls and a pizza box. And a frost-colored freezer envelope— of the sort used to store cutlets, thin meats wrapped in butcher paper. He'd used them for the same purposes as everyone else, I knew, but also for other more eccentric reasons: documents, scattered notes, travel papers, spare cash. Stashed up there in the freezer, where they would be safe until Armageddon. Or the next defrost cycle, whichever came first.

"We don't have much crime," he repeated.

"No."

"A baby one time, washed up on the beach."

The Russian stood gazing at the water. What he was thinking about, who could say? About the drowned baby? The neighborhood before the hurricane? The Widow Klinski? Or Maxwell Seeghurs and the lost rent he would never collect? Another minute I would be long gone, headed up Neptune

Avenue, past the Mermaid Walk, the minor league ballpark, the whole mildewed business.

He faced me.

"Dorothy," he said pointedly. "Dorothy Waters. I remember that one now, her name, looking at the sea, it come back."

I didn't follow.

"The woman on cot. Funny bird. She come, she go." He shrugged, glanced at his watch. Pleased with himself, his memory, that steel trap that let nothing go. The name itself, Dorothy Waters, didn't matter much to him otherwise, and right then it didn't mean much to me. "I have appointment. You come back later, fill out the paperwork. Otherwise . . ."

I could have left then, but I'd come all this way. Out of guilt, the need to expiate. Or some other ragged desire I didn't fully understand. Because people, once in motion, tend to stay that way. The place might have been cleaned out by Seeghurs himself before he bailed—but that didn't make sense. The suitcase was still here, also the freezer envelope. I wondered what else lay behind, in the unexamined spaces, or the basement below.

"If you don't mind, I'd like to spend a little time alone here, before deciding. Just a few minutes. To wander around. Feel the vibe."

"*The vibe*, yes," he repeated. The phrase amused him. "You a cop?"

"No."

"Detective?"

"No."

"I'll have hell to pay if your friend comes back, something's missing. Bad vibe. You understand? Big liability for me, let you wander all around."

The gesture he made, shrugging his heavy shoulders, both hands open, was almost apologetic. He was playing me, a small play, out of habit, or just to entertain himself, but over time, the small plays added up. I didn't want to be his entertainment, but I wanted a longer look.

I was about to reach in my wallet again when the Russian's cell rang.

How he answered—in a sweet, deep-throated voice, speaking a language I didn't understand—I knew then, if I had not guessed already, what lay between him and the widow.

He muted his cell.

I gave him the third twenty.

"You got a bargain."

"Sure."

"I take this call outside. You have your minutes with the house."

I went to the freezer first. To the frost-colored envelope with the folded butcher paper inside. I unfolded the butcher paper and found another envelope inside, and inside that a notebook with travel papers clipped to a letter bearing the insignia of Banco Internacional. Not a brilliant hiding place, the freezer, but sometimes the obvious slipped by.

I put the envelope on the counter.

Then examined the bathroom, pulled the dusty bookshelf from the wall, unbuckled Seeghurs' suitcase. The latter was full, the contents disarranged. If there had been anything of interest there, it was gone now.

I checked the drawers, inside the cabinets, beneath the bed, under the mattress.

The smell worsened. Maybe it was the exertion, or my nervousness, or my own rising stink in the confined space. I stepped onto the landing to get a breath. Out front, the Russian cooed into his cell. I could not see the beach—the sagging, ruined house blocked the view, but I could see over its roof to the further horizon, to the ocean, the gray swells that started way out there, breaking into whitecaps, troughing in the depths, then swelling again, and I could hear those swells as they broke and rushed onto the shore.

The Russian paced out of my view.

There was still the basement. I went back to the envelope on the counter—sliding its contents into the pocket of my cargo jacket. It might put Max in a bind, but I needed a closer look and was running out of time. He would do the same. I stepped back onto the landing, then went down the concrete stairs to the rear door of the storage garage. I pushed it open without much trouble. Caught the smell again, heavier now. Something went scampering. The gray light fell through the door, a shrinking light that creased the nearer wall with shadow. There was a slatted bench, chest high, and a darker shadow against the bench, a lumpen shadow: a form which, as my eyes sharpened, seemed to gain dimension, dangling like a misshapen sack. Except it wasn't a sack.

I groped for the light.

More skittering—away from the dangling figure into the depths of the garage. The man hung from the work bench, head tilted, legs splayed. He wore a leather jacket and jeans, an electric cord around his neck, cinched tight: the cord had been looped around a vise on the bench. His face was bloated, and rough hair fell into his eyes. I recognized the face, and could see the man had struggled, fingers trapped between the wire cord and his neck, trying to get loose. I am not an expert on forensics but judging from the smell—not as bad as it would be, not yet—Seeghurs had not been dead long. The animals scampered at the back of the garage, chittering about, the little bastards, impatient, not as afraid as one might hope. As I stepped forward, another rustled out from behind Seeghurs.

How it seemed, first glance, was he'd hung himself using the cord, securing it around the bench vise, then let the weight of his body do the rest. A clumsy job, not the old-fashioned kind of hanging, from the high rafters, executed with a kick of the chair out from underneath—but it was common enough. People hung themselves from shower heads, from doorknobs, tabletops, using ropes, scarves, bungee cords, phone wire. He had clawed his throat, trying to pry the cord lose—the natural instincts taking over—but gravity had brought him down, the length of the cord too short to allow him to either stand up or sit. He had strangled with his head flush to the table, his feet splayed at the knees.

The rats grew impatient along the edge of the wall. I heard the Russian on the other side of the garage, cooing away.

A bottle of whiskey balanced on the bench, an empty glass nearby. No note. So, he'd had a last drink, but nothing to say. The smell started to get to me. I gave Seeghurs a last hard look. He was scuffed up, dirty, as if he'd rolled around in the street, drunk, or fallen down the stairs on the way to the basement.

Something was wrong. Max, the man I knew, might be self-destructive, putting himself at risk and everyone around him . . .

But this?

The Russian fell quiet outside. I heard only the ocean thrumming, then another sound, mixed in, a car idling. The idling ceased and I caught two voices: the Russian again and a woman, the Widow Klinski, no doubt, crooning, barking, laughing, the pair of them carrying on in their thick Slavic tongue.

I climbed the stairs and went to the screen. The Russian caught sight of me over the convertible top, his eyes full of mirth, as the woman laughed, a careless laugh—reckless, full of some illicit beauty—a laugh that might have sparked in me some vicarious joy if not for that smell, which I still carried with me, along with the packet I'd taken from the freezer, too late to return now that the Russian had seen me. I stepped out onto the decaying porch.

HALF AN HOUR later, I moved at a hard clip on the Riegelmann Boardwalk. I had not intended to walk along the ocean to the subway terminus, but I'd been too shook up to mind directions. I'd taken the quickest path that got me out of sight of Voshki in the gatehouse.

I had not told the Russian about Seeghurs' body. I had not called the police. Perhaps I should have, but when I'd stepped onto the porch, the Russian approached me in the same manner as when I'd first arrived, guarded, with a hint of menace. Meanwhile, the Widow Klinski eased her car down the block.

"You look a little pale," he said.

I was tempted to blurt it out, to tell him about Seeghurs, but something held me back. I didn't trust the Russian.

"I've been traveling."

"What does that have to do with anything?"

"I get pale when I travel."

He put his hand on my shoulder, paternal. I trusted him even less.

"You need to eat."

I wondered if he knew about Seeghurs' body in the basement. If he had something to do with it—or knew who did—and had let me poke around below because he didn't want to be the one to call the police.

"So, you want to rent now—take over the lease?"

I'd all but forgotten our little ruse.

"I'll have to think about it," I said.

He frowned. Down the block, the Widow Klinski pulled her yellow car into the driveway of a two-story house, freshly painted. She was a statuesque woman, silver hair, flame white, and from the way she glanced at the Russian before heading up the stoop, and the way he glanced back, I could see I was falling down his list of priorities.

"All right. You think about. But if someone else comes along first, the application fee, it's non-refundable."

Tell him now, I told myself. *Or beat it. Get the fuck out.* He saw the thought pass through my head, but couldn't read me. His eyes narrowed.

"Non-refundable," he repeated.

After leaving the Russian, I had second thoughts. I should report the body. Get on the phone and call. In a few more steps, I'd be out of the gateman's sight, around the corner, away from Surf Street, another block, out of the wind coming off the ocean, past this group of kids in their black hoodies, these tattooed women in their beach robes, the snot-nosed old men drinking Rolling Rock on a bench. But with each step, the farther I walked, so grew the difficulty in explaining why I hadn't called from the scene, or what I'd been doing rummaging around in his things. Even an anonymous call would attract attention. The cops had the ability to capture phone numbers, ping the location of the call, even after you'd hung up. I kept walking, past the high-rise projects, down the long boardwalk through the suddenly cold summer evening, the dampening air, down to Luna Park. I wondered how long before the stench of the corpse attracted attention, what the Russian would tell the cops—how long before the police would trace me down. I headed for Stillwell Station. Past the Cyclone and the Ferris Wheel and the Freak Show; everything was closed, a chilly night, midweek, without much action, the steel doors pulled to the ground.

SIX

———

I GOT OFF the train in Midtown and walked to the Evangeline.

It was a small hotel with a small lobby, directly over the old Q line, and I could hear the subway rattling below.

I called home, Renée first, then my folks in Santa Rosa. No one picked up.

I knew Seeghurs' working mechanisms: the reporters' notebooks, full of scrawled notes, names intermixed with addresses and glancing descriptions. He avoided the digital world, or made a pretense of doing so, relying on others—the last few years it had been Anna—to be his fixers, to make his arrangements, to type his raw notes. Before he started drafting, he collected the material into notebooks, dated and numbered, arranged loosely by subject matter. Source books, he called them. The notebook I'd pulled from the freezer envelope was one of those source books, started early in the process.

It was hell to follow. Bits and pieces . . . old articles taped to the pages . . . colored charts with names, crisscrossed lines . . . more names . . . chapter outlines. Early thinking, rough stuff, abandoned, but revisited occasionally, judging from the annotations, the marginalia. Occasionally I ran across names I recognized, people with whom I'd had passing familiarity, some I'd worked with: a real estate lawyer, a lobbyist, a celebrity dogwalker, my blue-eyed client Jim Gaddis (the political riser who had his own glancing interactions with Sundial, more than glancing if I am honest). Not unexpected, given Gaddis's ambitions and the Sundial Foundation's status as a funder, and how the political worlds, the social, the celebrity, all overlapped.

There were other entries, seemingly haphazard, much of it fished from the public record, including the tabloids, focusing on details from Mikel Rolland's private life.

Old stuff, a tumble of gossip and alleged fact, hard to differentiate.

But there were also some dated entries, from a year back, about the time we'd been in Miscoulga. These concerned a young woman in North Omaha, the source he'd driven up to see: a youth counselor who worked with runaways, girls mostly, street kids in half-way homes.

It took a minute before it clicked: the name.

Dorothy Waters.

The Russian had pulled it from his memory while staring out at the Atlantic in Seeghurs' apartment. The woman on the cot. Dorothy Waters, also known as Valerie Hite, according to the notes in front of me: a young woman who in her earlier life had her own problems on the street. Charged with prostitution, drug possession, petty theft. Who'd had some interaction—Seeghurs' notes here being less legible—with Rolland's adopted son under her previous identity, down in Albuquerque. She and the son, Zeke Rolland, had been arrested together—charges dropped. By virtue of the boy's influential father.

Valeria Hite, aka Dorothy Waters.

What she had to do with Sundial, I couldn't see, but I knew Seeghurs' tendency to approach a story from the backdoor.

This means of entry had been Max's strength as a reporter, but also a weakness.

He found things others didn't.

There were also blind alleys, sometimes dangerous.

I went back to the envelope, the travel documents. The letter from Banco Internacional outlining access procedures for a cash account.

This wasn't unusual for Max.

He kept himself stashed, ready to travel.

There was something else, though, harder to figure.

A passport, not in his name.

An Australian document issued to one Maggie Highsmith of Melbourne: a dark-eyed woman with a mottled complexion.

An intriguing face, malleable features, neither attractive nor ugly—one you might forget if not for the eyes, all but black, and her ragged complexion. I examined the passport, an older one, without all the biometrics, not yet expired. Popular with forgers, I knew, because Seeghurs had told me. He knew how to secure them and had done so for himself, for tricky situations, and for others who needed to vanish.

I looked for Maggie Highsmith among those other names in Seeghurs' notebook, but it wasn't there.

I was missing something. I spread everything on the bed, went through it again. Something almost clicked but didn't. Whatever I was missing, I couldn't see.

▭

I made my way to a bar at the end of the block, a neighborhood place, not too busy, a woman just off work lingering over her phone, locals in the back, a mix of suits, young lovers kissing wearily in a corner booth. The place was not exclusive, neither upscale nor down. I liked this kind of moment, both away from the familiar and inside it, a quality I enjoyed about my work, the chance to escape, to fall below the radar and enter (however briefly) another life.

A train went by below, shaking the floor of the bistro.

I dialed Anna.

The phone went to voice mail.

The woman at the end of the bar lingered on. Her eyes met mine, flitted away. A window into another world that I had walked through on occasion, staring back at the empty seat in the world I'd left behind.

I wondered what else Anna might know.

The woman ordered another drink.

She gave me a glance, curious, open-eyed. The way she held herself—an invitation, maybe? Or a distraction, at least, a conversation, a way of getting Seeghurs out of my head. We regarded each other nakedly, nothing subtle about it, and it became clear—in the looking glass behind the bar—that whatever small intimacy might pass between us, the instant such intimacy expired the other person would cease to exist. Her drank came and I turned away from the mirror. I should go back to the hotel, I told myself. Run everything from Seeghurs' place through the shredder in the business room off the lobby. Be rid of Max.

But I wasn't ready to do that.

I went to the subway.

I'd had a little too much to drink and could hear the blood moving in my head. The whispering in the tunnels past and present . . . the muttering of Italian masons . . . the Mohawk ironworkers . . . the Jamaican whores . . . the Dutch bankers interred in the tombs overhead, still counting their possessions ... runaway slaves . . .

The car grew more congested as it approached the river, the light dimmer, the air sulfurous and stale.

SEVEN

▭

I RODE THE N-line under the East River, to lower Astoria, getting off at Thirty-Third under the racket of the el. Queens had upscaled, especially close in, but here, depending on your compass, it was still easy enough to walk through the thin line of gentrification into something sketchier. Anna's place was in an older six-plex, not particularly well kept, in a no-man's land between the restored row houses and the glass complexes that looked across the river toward Manhattan.

When I buzzed, no one answered.

Her apartment, on the upper floor, was dimly lit, if at all— maybe a light in the back, or just a reflection. A brighter light tumbled from the apartment next door. The woman who lived there, Kate, I'd met once: a slatternly blonde who'd known what was going on between us and wasn't judgmental. The three of us had spent a few hours together on the small rooftop patio, drinking and eating.

I rang again, first Anna's buzzer, then the other. It took a bit, but Kate answered. The lock on the main door appeared new, but the intercom was faulty, full of static.

"Who is this?"

I told her.

"Who?"

I told her again. She didn't remember me at first, then she did.

"Just a moment."

She came down the stairs, a bit wobbly, a graphic designer who spent most of her time alone.

"I'm afraid Anna isn't here."

"Working late?"

"Thursday night. Her job, they've got her on the road. So, she's been doing long weekends lately. A lot of time in Philly."

No doubt the two of them had talked me over. Kate's expression went quizzical. Trying to figure me out. A married man. A fling, the kind she'd had herself. *More than once.* She'd said as much, half-drunk, up there on the rooftop. *Always, those things end so sadly, especially the ones that are any fun to begin with.*

"Why are you here?"

"I need to talk to her."

"She's moved on."

"It's business. Something I've been working on."

"You should have called."

"I was in the neighborhood."

"To be honest, I don't see her so much. Her work, her life. Home a couple days, then gone again, never mind the break-in. What it takes before the landlord fixes the goddamn lock. Sons-of-a-bitches, just yesterday. Strolled right into her apartment. Middle of the day."

"Break-in?"

"Just Anna's place. Lucky girl, she wasn't home. I was, music on, didn't hear a thing. Scary, but they didn't take much. A bit of jewelry, sentimental value. And that old laptop, the one Anna used for her ex—broken Wi-Fi, old software, compatible with nothing." She shook her head. "Junkies, my guess. Take anything. Who the hell would want that?"

"What about Max Seeghurs?" I asked, though it occurred to me, if the break-in had been so recent, Seeghurs was already dead.

"No, he had a key. Anyway, she'd given him an ultimatum, a few weeks back—about getting his stuff out. She didn't want to be involved anymore. No more hazard duty," she laughed. I'd heard the phrase before, how Anna referred to Max, half-joking. "I don't know. Anna was spooked. Went off to Philly this morning, early train. Off to see her person. Another working weekend, how she put it."

"Her person?"

She pursed her lips, wry. "Some congressman, out of Harrisburg."

I suddenly envisioned Max how I'd last seen him, in the basement in Coney Island. I felt the compulsion to tell Kate—to tell someone, anyone, get that image out of my head—but I knew better. Kate saw my distress, mistaking its source, and dismissed me gently.

"I'll tell her you stopped by."

▭

I TALKED TO Fred from the airport the next morning.

I described the scene for him, the abandoned beach house, the ocean, the landlord, the suitcase by the bed—suggesting Seeghurs had been about to leave, or just returned, it was hard to say. I didn't mention the basement. The body.

"No manuscript?"

"No."

"You looked in the refrigerator."

"Yes."

I didn't mention the envelope I'd taken either. Evidence tampering, the cops would say. Fred didn't need to know.

"How about his ex?"

"She's out of town."

"With him?"

"No. She's a got a new boyfriend. In Philly."

"So, he's disappeared."

"He does that, doesn't he?"

"Maybe something happened."

"Maybe."

"We could file a missing person report."

"What good will that do?"

"Check the hospitals," said Fred. "Asylums, whorehouses."

"He'll show up," I lied.

"So, we're empty-handed. No manuscript, no writer, no nothing."

I didn't say anything.

"This fucks me over," Fred said. "Word gets around."

I got on the plane. Thought about Renée, our kids, nestled in our house the other side of country. I remembered Seeghurs' assertions, his fear he was being followed—watched. I felt the fear, too, contagious, but no one paid me any mind. I was just another person on a plane. Up here, in the clouds, whatever happened in the cellars of Brooklyn had nothing to do with me. I slept. Back home, the air came in from the coast, a mild breeze. Renée kissed me, her tongue deep in my mouth. Everything was fresh and clean.

PART 3

HOME

EIGHT

WORKING WITH CLIENTS inevitably involves a certain amount of sparring. With some it's purely verbal, others more physical. You must allow yourself to be beaten—at tennis, racquetball, golf —whatever it might be, but not too easily. Gaddis liked to run. I had gone for a jog with the candidate a few months back, down the coast, at his family place on the beach. He'd done most of the talking, his blue eyes focused on the horizon, then broken into a hard sprint at the end. Since then, I'd been going out more regularly on my own, jogging up the hill, past the patches of milkweed where my daughter collected larvae for her butterfly project.

I entered the tunnel, a path under the freeway near the homeless camp, itself tucked away in the eucalyptus trees behind the Civic Center. I ran a loop, the last stretch a bit ragged, through the commuter lot where a missing teenager from Wyoming had been found in the trunk of an abandoned Chevy.

"I bumped into Margaret Styles last night," said Renée.

She leaned against the refrigerator, dressed for work, for the courthouse, the more mundane part of her job, translation of testimony in corporate lawsuits. The case concerned a French jet—designed in the Silicon Valley—that had gone down over the Atlantic.

"How's Margaret doing?"

I hadn't told Renée about Seeghurs, no more then I'd told Fred. I didn't want to involve her.

"She just got done with a party fundraiser. Out at the Domes."

The Domes Mansion anchored the embassy end of Pacific Heights. The owner threw parties, a mix of artists and bohemians and socialites, and occasionally these things took on a political cast. There'd been a time when I'd been more of a presence. And carried, too, I liked to imagine, the scent of celebrity myself.

"She'd liked to talk to you," said Renée.

"About what?"

"Something to do with Gaddis. His campaign. She was a bit coy, how she always is. Friendly though. And curious about what you were up to in New York."

"You told her."

"Don't worry, I was coy too."

▭

I'D BEEN TO the Sundial House a couple years back, not long before everything went to hell, and mingled alongside that black-bottom pool in the Santa Fe hills. I'd come as the guest of an aging screen star, an animal-rights activist. I was ghostwriting an article about her devotion to desert habitat.

I'd seen Mikel Rolland then. He was in a spiritualist phase, not long after his wife's death—his ragged looks gone more ragged: a thin, harrowed man, once vibrant, who seemed on the edge of disappearing.

"You work with Jim Gaddis." It wasn't a question. Rather statement of fact, laconic, hard to read, maybe just weariness, all those people mingling, looking for a piece of him.

The conversation didn't go much further.

"Don't take it personally," said the actress. "Mikel, he's withdrawn as of late. More and more. Out to Taos, his ranch there."

In communion with the goats and the apples. Also, a peyote shaman who maintained a kiva on the property.

Increasingly disenchanted with Sundial, at odds with the board.

That was the rumor.

How much was true, I didn't know, though it wasn't hard to sense—among the minglers there was a palpable and creeping disillusionment. Still glamour in the air, but a dark glamour.

I'd also glimpsed his adopted son, Zeke Rolland. Dead now—like his father—but still on the coil that night, rubbing elbows at the fringes, lounging, dissolute, in proximity with a handful of others, who seemed to want to maintain that proximity, drinks in hand, talking a bit louder than they should have. They'd wandered away after a bit, down the hall, accompanied by a couple of women, richly dressed, younger, who appeared bored out of their minds.

"Things used to be more wholesome around here," the actress said. "Or at least more discreet."

"It's all right."

"They like people to gawk. But you didn't come here for that."

"Maybe I did."

She laughed, introduced me around. Mostly people of like mind, her eco-friends, as she called them—people she'd worked with, actors in her story—but not all. Among the latter, a new board member, a lawyer taking the place of another lawyer from the same firm, offices on K Street in DC. Corporate clients, politicians, lobbying groups. Also, foreign nationals, donors interested in real estate, attracted to Sundial's urban redevelopment projects, initiatives that relied on a blend of private and public money.

Gaddis had been instrumental in a number of these, waterfront projects mostly—American River, Long Beach, San Francisco. I'd helped him on some of the spin, when the China Basin project gutted some old residency hotels.

It had gotten messy.

I'd whispered it away, the worst of it. (Misdirection, more accurately. Rumors about old clients, some true, spilled over cocktails to my colleagues in the press.) The legal end had been handled by that same firm that rotated its lawyers onto the Sundial board, closely affiliated with Cole & Clark in whose Sacramento office that young intern had worked before being discovered in the mud by the river.

Gaddis's name had been circled in Max's notebook.

So had a lot of others.

Government officials, construction firms, party regulars, intelligence operatives, politicians, prostitutes.

Whose relationship to one another seemed tangential at best.

It was hard to tell Max's logic.

If he'd been sober. Or just sifting his notes, early on.

Now I sifted, too.

I ended up online, at the conspiracy sites.

More names.

Crown princes.

Criminal overlords, corporate executives.

Ex-presidents, their wives, children, dogs.

Convicted pedophiles.

Astronauts.

Linked by an associative logic that went up the social ladder, and down. And eventually dragged in just about everyone.

Including myself. In an article cited by the Drudge Report, identified as an ex-journalist working as a mercenary for people on either side of the political spectrum, a hired gun for the illuminati. I'd seen the article before, and the accompanying photograph. Captioned to juxtapose my real name alongside my changing pseudonyms. I'd been listed with influential people, some of whom I admired, others not so much. I'd been amused at first, flattered, but that info had spread to other sites—Freemasons, Zorroists, Reptilians—so I'd hired someone to have my name scrubbed, or at least pushed to the darker corners of the web.

I contemplated the article now, the photo—my image shape shifting in the digital shadow—and wondered for a moment just who I might really be.

I called Margaret Styles, the handler Renée had run into at the Domes—who these days worked for Hastings & Hastings, a political consulting firm hired recently by the Gaddis campaign. I'd done work for the Hastings group: hatchet work on a Republican candidate, a Hispanic woman who, because of my research, had lost her district when news of an abortion came out late in her campaign.

"I hear you've been traveling."

"Just a little," I said. "New York. Also, DC."

The latter wasn't true, but I didn't mind her thinking so.

"Has anyone roped you in yet?"

"Just meetings."

"You met with the Morales campaign?"

I hesitated,

A long beat.

Preoccupied with Seeghurs, I'd lost touch with the campaign wire. But I knew Angela Morales, a defense attorney who'd battled her way out of the Central Valley. She was running for Senate now. On the surface, she was no threat to Gaddis, at least not immediately: same party, same slate, running for a different office. At the same time, Morales had grassroots support, an overlapping base, and the Gaddis people were nervous about her long term, on the national stage. They both had further ambitions.

"That's confidential," I said. Truth was, there'd been no contact—but I knew the advantage of being desired elsewhere.

"We'd prefer you with us."

"That's where I'd love to be."

"Gaddis is a good man."

"Yes."

"He's on the right side of history."

"Yes," I agreed, and kept the ambivalence out of my voice. It was the kind of thing people in campaigns tended to say. In reality, the world is an ambiguous place. Everybody knows. It's hard to tell what is good, what is evil, and my job was to mask that ambivalence. My father was a scientist and had insisted, in the big scheme of things, that all fact was casual, sufficient to get this or that accomplished in certain situations—but the notion of Incontrovertible Truth was a matter of convenience, bound to particular realities. Meanwhile, certain practical things had to be done.

I took some solace in this.

"As much as we love Angela, and the passion she stirs, she has some trouble outside the base—also, there are ugly rumors. Not that we believe them." Why this came up, I didn't grasp right away, but I did later. I'd done quite a bit of ghost work for Morales's mentor, a brawling black politician who'd died a couple years back. So, I'd been witness to her rise. I knew things.

"Of course, she has our unequivocal support."

"Everyone loves Angela," I said. "But the future of the party, it's Jim Gaddis." I stopped there, not wanting to overplay. "If there's anything I can do . . ."

"We were just talking about you, some of the ideas you and Jim discussed. He'd like a chance to sit down, but his schedule—" She cut herself short. "Let me get back to you as soon as the dust clears."

They were fishing, I thought, vetting me. A good sign, maybe. Or it could be they just wanted to keep me near.

Renée and I languored in the infinity pool. We touched fingers, kissed. She still wore makeup from work, and I tasted the pale gloss on her lips.

It was a dark night, no moon.

She wore a white swimsuit, a two-piece, and drifted with her head back.

I put my hand under her suit.

"I have a call to make," she said.

"No you don't."

"I do."

"Who?"

"The French."

We lingered in the water. An animal moaned in the brush. I kissed her neck, her shoulders. She touched me softly, her eyes on that place where the water fell off the edge into the black sky. I looked, too. Put my hand on her stomach. Our legs interlaced. Later, she climbed out and I watched her put on a white robe in the darkness, a sheer robe that caught the light.

She went inside.

I wanted to follow, but I couldn't just yet. I dried myself and sat on the chaise lounge with my illuminated tablet. Then checked the blotter out of Brooklyn.

There was nothing on the wire.

Nothing on Seeghurs, nothing out of Coney. If his body had been discovered, the police were keeping it to themselves.

NINE

MY FATHER DEVELOPED a problem with his eyes. He had trouble blinking. A form of palsy caused—or so the doctor speculated—by an ischemic stroke, or a pinched nerve, or an insect bite. A spider, perhaps, or a tick. A condition, the doctor assured us, that would pass on its own, after some indefinite time. Or not pass at all.

"So, did you accomplish your business?" my father asked. We sat in the sun. "During your travels, I mean."

A car drove by, an ordinary car, nothing special about it. We fell silent. Their recent visitors, my mother's call to Renée, went undiscussed. Their living situation—what was real, imagined, misperceived—could be hard to sort. I didn't want to stir things up.

"Travel isn't always about accomplishment," my mother said.

"We traveled a lot," my father said. "That's correct. We did that." He shielded his brow, putting his eyes in shadow. His speech slurred less than before, as if one ailment had canceled the other. "Though of course there's not much difference between here and there." He wasn't talking about culture, but distance, about light, wave particles. Things he had spent his life studying. "Time," he said. He dropped the hand from his face. His cognition came and went. "This time, that time, all times." He pointed at my phone. "The psychical dimension is an illusion. Meaningless." He coughed, his voice sputtering. "Except for this one," he tapped his chest. "The one we're trapped in. But the mind . . ." He leaned back, retreating into himself, struggling for the thread.

"It turns to jelly," my mother said.

"Yes." My father blinked. Once. "Electricity does not travel well through a viscous substance. One part of the brain loses contact with the other . . . but it doesn't mean, necessarily, we have ceased to exist . . . our consciousness . . ."

My parents had traveled all over. They'd been to great underground ruins and modern missile portals and sat in village taverns guarded by men with machine guns. Towns full of old people they now resembled, leather-skinned and shrunken, members of an ancient race whose memories were communicated by their presence, like artifacts dug up out of the ground.

"They treated us like royalty. Your father, especially, they treated him like some lost son." My mother, when speaking of my father, demonstrated (intentionally or otherwise) a remarkable gift for mixing pride with resentment. "But you . . . you . . ."

"It's okay, mom."

I pushed their attention toward the food I'd picked up at a burger joint near the casino in Cotati.

"Fried chicken . . ." my father said.

I had intended to buy some but remembered the doctor's cautions about bones.

"Next time."

"Deep fried. A breast with wings."

The hamburger sat in its wrapper on the table. My mother hadn't touched her onion rings. I'd gotten her a Slurpee, strawberry.

"This tastes like blood," she said.

It was late, the sun setting. My father ran his tongue over his lips—then went still, eyes wide, impossibly so.

Incipient scleroderma, the doctor had speculated, tests unconfirmed. A nervous condition, not well understood, possible hereditary, that culminated in a scabrous transformation of the body.

"I can feel them out there."

"It's okay, Mom."

It was an old refrain, ringing back to my childhood—when my father had been a young man in a white shirt, in a military neighborhood, the creeks full of crawfish, and the streets under patrol, Russian agents, whomever, spies and counterspies, and it was true, some years back, I'd done some ghost work for a former CIA agent, a whistleblower, whose work had overlapped in a marginal way with my father's, and security had come to talk to me, too, but it had all been pro forma, blowhard stuff. Whatever information my father might have had, it was old, antiquated, and my whistleblower had died of a heart attack before telling me much. I'd written the book anyway, *My Life as A Spy,* using information the agency had given me, obvious malarkey, but it had done well.

We fell quiet. There was no traffic. We dawdled for a while, then I wheeled my parents inside. I drummed up the volume on the set, so my mother might hear.

"What's on?"

"The news."

"About the war?"

"I can change the channel."

"Which war?"

I couldn't tell. Syria, maybe, or Afghanistan, or that new business in the Donbas. There were flares illuminating a night sky, bodies on the ground. Children emerging from chemical gas. Or not emerging. A sniper outside a shopping mall in San Bernardino.

"I'll change the channel."

"It's okay," my mother said. "I like to stay current."

"How about the cooking show? That man you like, the chef who travels all over the world?"

"He died," my mother said.

"Oh."

"One week he's there, the next . . . Well, it ended badly, you know. All that food, it depressed him."

"I didn't know."

"Corn . . . String beans . . . You know how it is."

"Mashed potatoes," my father said.

"Yes."

I felt badly about the chicken.

"Put on what you like. I can't see anyway—and your father, the noise reassures him."

They drifted off, my father first, eyes still open, but snoring, then my mother, blind as a bat. It grew dark outside, then darker, and after a while it was just the glow from the flat screen, falling across our faces, the sound of urgent voices, explosions, politicians on the stump (midterm maneuvering, senate seats, state elections), a babble replaced as the evening went along with talk shows, old comedies, laugh tracks, medication warnings, erectile enhancements. It was oddly comforting, sedating. I fell asleep, too, then woke at the creaking of the front door, footsteps in the hall, big footsteps, not Mazie their caretaker—but her husband and her son, recently arrived from Fiji, big people, like Mazie herself, come from far away, across the ocean, to wheel my parents off to bed.

"Your father likes to talk."

"Sometimes," I said.

So, these were my mother's spies. Mazie's husband had a stump at the wrist: chromosome damage passed on from his own father, a soldier who'd died from radiation poisoning after serving with the Brits at Bikini Atoll. The pair bantered.

"Your mother's a good woman."

"Wife of important man."

"Very important"

"Wise."

The son put his thumbs next to my father's eyes, one on each side, on the ridge by the temple. "Touch here. Very gentle, and eyes close by themselves. We see it sometimes on our islands. Among the Degei."

The Degei were caretakers of a shrine at the center of the islands, built on a volcanic fissure through which the ancestral people (part human, part something else) had emerged at the dawn of time.

I was skeptical.

Nonetheless, my father seemed to respond. His lids relaxed. His face fell into a state of repose.

—

It was late by the time I got home, the house quiet, the air balmy and sweet. I could smell the jasmine and the pinyon and the dry grass. Renée hadn't returned yet. The kids were still up. I'd seen the lights in the windows when I'd driven in, then stood for a while looking up at the house, the white clouds drifting through the black sky. A night breeze came from the hills, through the window slats in our bedroom. I lay on my back, the ceiling fan spinning overhead, one hand off the edge of the bed and the other sprawled out toward Renée's side, where she usually lay—then I woke with a start, not realizing until that moment I'd been asleep at all. I checked the street, then my kids. The light glowed under my daughter's door, but inside she lay curled asleep, under a poster of a giant butterfly. Down the hall, my son worked away on his computer, teaming with kids on the other side of the country, in the virtual elsewhere, killing giant insects who emerged from caves in the center of the world.

I let him be.

I went downstairs and contemplated the cage in the backyard where my daughter kept her butterfly experiment. Several pupas hung on the milkweed she'd cultivated. She was an odd kid, a bit of a loner, dedicated in her solitude to the monarchs, to the unfolding of their wings, the sudden bright escape from the cage. Renée rolled up. I recognized the sound of the car. I saw her headlights sweep the hill and heard the engine die in the driveway.

Her face was flushed, and she looked happy.

"You should have come."

"Where?"

"To the opera."

"You didn't say anything."

"I texted."

"I was in Santa Rosa."

"Don't worry, it was a last-minute thing, opening night, embassy tickets—and Rouche was in town. You know how they are."

I did know how they were, especially opening nights, when the house filled with celebrities and politicos, and I knew Rouche Industries—a French start-up, bio tech—was looking to establish political ties.

"Gaddis stopped by our box," she said.

I felt a small rush. This news surprised me, though only for an instant. It was election season. People passed in and out of the boxes, tarried at the back, shook hands, drank champagne. Of course, Rouche would want to meet Gaddis, and the other way around. No doubt there'd been others nosing by: Pelosi; Whitman; the crew from Oracle; also, Ryckman; Giannini; Condoleezza—the list went on. It was the kind of event, in the past, I would have gone—but half the people, I'd worked for them at one point, or against them. So, spending an evening inside one of those small boxes, at the War Memorial Opera House—given the secrets I knew, the lines I had to walk—wasn't the easiest thing.

"He stuck around for a bit."

I imagined Jim Gaddis, that dark hair swept back, the blue eyes, the charge he brought to a room. People were drawn to him. He enjoyed it, and that drew them more.

"Did you talk?"

"Part of my job—but it was enjoyable. He's bright enough. He's got some charisma, anyway."

"He does."

"He seemed to know quite a bit about our trade with the French. But he wasn't glib. He listened. Also, what I hear, he's way ahead in the polls."

"It's still early."

"I know, but he doesn't have any real opposition."

When Renée and I first met, our talk had been all about making the world a better place. Commerce, the exchange of coin, facilitated the exchange of ideas. All it took was gathering around the table. Commodity—in the legislature, as in the marketplace—was at the heart of all discourse. Only the miserly insisted otherwise. The eventual realization, which seemed at first a delicious secret, was that it all happened in back rooms. As in the market, strewn with paper, pig guts, blood-stained ledgers, it was there, behind closed doors, where things were parsed and divided, legislation written. It thrilled her, too, being at the center of the deal. We were both interpreters, though of different sorts. I'd enjoyed watching Renée in the early days, and now, too, here in our kitchen, in her white blouse and pearls and lipstick, glamorous, irresistible. "He embraces the need for foreign investment."

"Did he offer *you* a job?"

"No," she said. "He hasn't been elected yet."

"But he will."

"He thinks so, too." She laughed. That was the knock on Gaddis. He regarded himself as inevitable.

"He spoke about you. About your jog together, along the beach."

She leaned away, her head in profile, smiling to herself—as if no longer aware of my presence. Remembering some moment from the evening, some small exchange. She pursed her lips, her eyes spidered, the laugh lines, the frown lines, the long days at court, nights on the town, all made themselves evident. I kissed her on the neck. She didn't mind. She smelled like the inside of a martini glass—of the twenty-odd years we'd spent together. I liked the feel of her against me. Her skirt had a slit on one side, and I ran my hand over her midriff, toying with the pleat.

"I get the feeling the door is open with Gaddis. This is a golden opportunity. He's in it for the long term. He's looking for people." I saw what she was thinking; he might hire us both. "You don't have to love him to work for him."

"I'll have to pretend."

"That's never stood in your way before."

The vulnerability spooled in her eyes, as if she knew every lie I'd ever told her. "We could throw this all over. If that's what you want."

"That's an idea."

"We could take the kids with us. We could go live in a hut."

She didn't mean it, but she kissed me as if she did, drawing me to her. She put her tongue in my ear, whispered something obscene, held me at arm's length.

"We are all culpable," she said. I put my hand on her thigh. "There's no point in letting it ruin your life."

TEN

<hr>

THE CALL CAME from Brooklyn, a female officer from Seagate Station. She had a drawling, squalid voice that reminded me of Coney Island, of the boardwalk and the gulls. Listening to her, I imagined the dawn out East—that gray sky growing pale over the police mobile unit inside Seagate—and heard at the same time the neighborhood in her voice: a voice that conjured dirty sand washing up against the sea wall, a Jew Puerto Rican Italian sound, too loud, at once prideful and full of self-disgust, but trying, at the moment, to show some bit of deference.

"Mr. Reynolds?"

"Yes."

"You have acquaintance with a Mr. Maxwell Seeghurs?"

I wasn't sure I wanted to admit this, but I had little choice. The officer came out with the reason she had called. I already knew, but it hit me anyway, same as it had when I recognized the figure hanging in his basement.

Seeghurs was dead, she told me.

They'd made the identification. The landlord, though, had

been unable to provide information as to next of kin, and the usual checks hadn't been fruitful. This baffled me, but I knew Seeghurs' first wife had remarried and put an ocean between them—and his marriage to Anna had taken place in Mexico. Maybe it wasn't on the books. Or maybe they were just doing what neighborhood cops did, going with what they had: the business card I'd left with Voshki at the front gate.

What the Sergeant wondered—and she repeated it, with that yawn in her mouth, a sadness, an inextricable boredom—was could I help out with something more definitive regarding next of kin.

"He was in the process of divorce. His second. She lives in Queens."

"What was your relationship to him?"

I hawed.

"Old friends. He was a colleague."

I told her why I'd gone out to see him, an abbreviated version. I figured the truth worked best. Not the whole truth, of course, as this was seldom a good idea.

"He'd been through some things lately."

"He was distraught?"

"I never got to speak to him. He hadn't been around the apartment for a while. At least that's what the landlord told me."

She had to know this. It would be in the report. Their office was right there in Seagate. They'd talked to the Russian, and to Voshki at the gate. They'd been called to the scene when the stench got too much. A neighbor's dog had gotten off leash, she explained. "Into the back there, under the fence—a poodle. He wouldn't stop barking."

She wanted to tell the story but checked herself. I asked the obvious.

"How did he die?"

Police could be tight with such information. I didn't know if she'd answer. She turned formal, as if speaking a different language, reading from a coroner's report. "Cerebral hypoxia. Induced by compression of the carotid artery and the breathing tube—" Her voice faltered, bungling it. "I'm sorry," she said. "He hung himself in the basement."

"Oh."

"Suicide, initial ruling," she said. I heard someone speak in the office behind her, indecipherable. The gray light of the Atlantic poured through the phone. "The Bureau wants to take a second look."

"The FBI?"

"They've taken an interest. Some history there, I guess. But my job, here, is to find the next of kin. Someone to make arrangements."

She wanted Anna's information. I hesitated. The way the cop had given me the news, I couldn't say it was out of the manual. Most police, what I'd seen—covering the beat in Sacramento—weren't that well-trained in passing on news of death. Those who'd had the experience didn't relish it and tended to shrug the duty down the line.

"We'll send someone out. From Queen's, that precinct, the hundred and fourth," she said.

"She's on the road, I believe. Quite a bit."

"We misconnect, I'm afraid. Well, Mr. Seeghurs could languish in the morgue. There's a daily charge."

How it worked out, I made the call.

Some residual sense of responsibility. Or because I wanted to hear Anna's voice.

I stepped outside, by the monarch cage, and left the best message I could. Then I went back and lay on the couch. I still lay there a couple of hours later, in the West Coast dawn, when my phone vibrated. On the other end, Anna was subdued, oddly calm, too calm, already skipping ahead to the service, not in New

York, she was thinking, but in Miscoulga. Because he was from the Midwest originally, never comfortable on the coasts, not really, and had an attachment to that muddy retreat on the Platte. I kept waiting for her to collapse, to weep, to let loose.

"He envied you," she said. "Your stable life. The people you worked with. Also, the fact, maybe when you got down to it—the work you did, from inside . . . it accomplished more . . ."

"I don't know about that."

"Well, he despised you, too."

She laughed. Seeghurs and I, our friendship had always cut two ways. I thought back to that last night in Miscoulga, our conversation, and for a moment was overcome.

"Will you come?"

"Of course."

When I got off the phone, I saw Renée standing in the shadows, in her nightgown, at the bottom of the staircase. I wondered how long she'd been there.

"Who was that?"

"Max Seeghurs died. I need to go to his memorial."

She sat next to me on the couch, just sitting. "You two were close, back then. That story, the law intern—her murder . . . it sent you in different directions."

Slowly the dawn fell away. The sky changed, and the light grew stark.

"Who was that on the phone?" she asked again.

I went to our sliding door and looked out at the long shadows in the morning light.

"His wife."

"Poor woman."

"Ex, I mean."

"Still."

Fred called. News traveled fast in the city, mercilessly so. The smartphones were relentless. Fred was shook up. He'd been fond of Max, despite their difficulties—but he had to be professional.

"There are loose ends."

Earlier he'd talked to an obit writer, he told me. Saying the pretty things one was supposed to say. Also, to Max's editor. Who, all things considered, seemed less devastated than relieved.

"Not everyone feels that way. He had fans. Still does."

"Of course."

"There are loose ends," he repeated.

One of these involved me. Potentially, at least. Fred had just gotten off the phone with an editor at an old-line magazine that had survived the digital purge. Seeghurs had promised an excerpt from *Sundial*.

"They need something to fill the spot," Fred said. "Something on Seeghurs himself. Touch on the unfinished story, what he was working on, but more on the paradox of the man . . . from a personal perspective."

I'd done something similar for the magazine before, but as a ghost: a piece under the name of an American diplomat who'd lost a colleague to a terror bombing. Their relationship had been a complex one, and certain things were best left in the shadows. The editor liked Fred's pitch: a ghost—a political fixer—writing about an old friend from the other side of the professional divide.

The advantage, for me, I could wash it any way I pleased.

Meanwhile—regarding Max's death—the online squibs all echoed the same line: suicide. Maybe the cop had spoken prematurely about the Bureau investigation, and the Feds had let it go. Or were holding their cards close.

"A byline, that magazine," Fred said. "Still carries some prestige."

I was not immune to such lures. Neither were my clients, so long as I stayed out of the muck, and kept them out too. Also, it was one of the slicks that still paid, with an upscale demographic, cultural sophisticates (or pretense to such), who liked it on their coffee tables.

"Unless you feel too close . . . they have their stable."

"No, no," I said. Their in-house people were good at what they did—soft news with an intellectual veneer—but there were some old school hounds there, the type who couldn't help pushing their snouts into every corner. I didn't want them on this. "He was my friend. If someone is going to memorialize him, it should be me."

PART 4

MISCOULGA

ELEVEN

Midwest, High Summer

THERE WERE THUNDER anvils rising north of Omaha. I could
see them from the Eppley Hotel, a brick low-rise on the wrong
side of the freeway, opposite downtown. It was an older estab-
lishment, without a lot to recommend it, but it provided a good
view up 24th Street, the former main street that ran through the
black neighborhood for several miles before disappearing into a
swelter of cottonwoods. Farther out, the clouds rose above the
prairie: a dark mass creased with heat lightning. Here, the sun
shone directly overhead, and the planes glinted as they circled in
over the Missouri.

The airport had reopened. The night before, my flight had
been delayed. There'd been storms all over the Midwest. By the
time I landed, it was well after midnight, too late to drive to
Miscoulga. Anna had been diverted to Chicago, and Seeghurs'
service had been pushed to the next afternoon.

It might have been wise for me to drive south, given the

break in the weather, but I had no appetite for sitting around Miscoulga.

Also, I knew Dorothy Waters—the youth counselor who'd spent some time on Max's cot in Brooklyn—lived over the line in North Omaha. Dorothy Waters, aka Valerie Hite, who in her earlier life had hung with Mikel Rolland's troubled son on the strip down in Albuquerque.

I idled in the parking lot next to the Eppley, along a worn stretch under the freeway—lined with soot-stained buildings, the color of lead—and waited for the air-conditioning to kick in. Then I crossed over into North Omaha. Dorothy Waters' address was on the other side of Highway 75, a mottled neighborhood, variously maintained: a small house behind a larger house at the end of a gravel drive.

The little house was empty, a FOR RENT sign in the window. I called the number, but the landlady was not nearly as talkative as the Russian in Coney Island. So, I sought out Dorothy Waters' place of employment, a safe house for young women occupying an old apartment building nearby, stone gray, on a flag lot next to the freeway. The house mother wasn't cooperative either.

"Miss Waters doesn't work here anymore."

As to the rest—the how, the when, the why—or where she might have gone, I might as well have been talking to the cottonwoods out back.

———

I could have let it go. The day was cloying, the humidity stuffing itself like a wet rag down my throat. Dorothy Waters had known something about Sundial, maybe (the source Fred had mentioned, the missing piece), though odds were, whatever she knew, it wasn't the end blow Max had been seeking.

She was too far off on the fringe.

Either way, I wasn't after an end blow. I could find some other way into the magazine piece. Grab color from these streets. Entwine the past, other places. Create froth out of nothing.

I was good at that kind of thing.

I walked from the safe house back to my car. Down the block, in my rearview, a grey sedan lumbered by the curb.

I grew contemplative in front of the blank windows of the safe house. Wondered what I was looking for.

I knew the old truism: a quest has little to do with the object pursued. Rather it begins and ends with the seeker.

I thought about Seeghurs, hanging from the short bench.

Glanced in the rearview.

It was bright overhead, but behind me, to the north, dark clouds mushroomed on the horizon.

The grey sedan had moved on.

Seeghurs' notes on Omaha were slim, a few names, places, jottings he'd made (according to his marginalia) while sitting at Stev's Barbeque, a local joint over on North Main. I swung by Stev's: the kind of local hangout Max and I had once sought out in the field, at the end of a long day in the Central Valley, chasing leads that went nowhere, finding solace in our failure—dust in our nostrils, the twang of the locals—and imagining that moment, when, if only for an instant, truth became sensate, palpable, a smell in the air, a taste. I was tempted to go inside Stev's, but it was still early. Anna wouldn't land for hours, and I had no appetite.

Meanwhile, there wasn't much else in Max's Omaha notes worth following.

A woman, maybe, name of Akeesha Aimsley, whose church

Waters had attended, and who ran a small insurance agency just down the block.

Ms. Aimsley was out of the office, according to a sign on the door.

Due back later this afternoon.

So, I drove to the New Hope Community Center where Waters had once volunteered. It occupied a defunct Savings & Loan in a working-class neighborhood not far away, upriver from the old smelter. An anonymous building, concrete gray. On the other side of the cottonwoods, a handful of kids loitered in front of a small grocery. They ignored me.

A car pulled up across the street, a featureless vehicle, color-less—washed out, grey, maybe, dirty blue—not dissimilar to the one I'd seen loitering by the safe house. Identical, maybe, if one accounted for the light, the blistering haze. I hadn't gotten a look at the driver, but I did now: a pale man in shades and a straw fedora. The kids retreated, ditching around the corner. The man gave me blasé glance, a threat underneath, I don't know.

The car rolled a bit farther, then stopped under the shade of one those big cottonwoods.

Years back, when I'd covered crime for *The Register*, I'd carried a short barrel Glock for a few months. I had never gotten used to carrying it—the weight, the feel, the uneasy thrill—and settled on a thimble shot of pepper spray on a key chain in my pocket. I didn't carry that anymore either, but retained the nervous habit, years later, of reaching toward my pocket in situations like this one.

Whether that gesture was wise or not, I don't know, but I made it now, and felt the hollow space.

The man turned away, gazing toward the corner the kids had left behind. A turf dick, maybe, on the juvenile beat, gang detail, probation officer—unconcerned with me, it seemed, but tracking me in his rearview out of habit, because that's what turf dicks did. I turned my back on him and made my way across the asphalt lot, under the New Hope sign, past an asbestos warning on the entry.

Inside the building, the central hall had been painted red and green, the Pan-African flag next to the Stars and Stripes, a community board papered with local events, the far corridor off limits, an asbestos warning pasted to a sawhorse. A tackboard featured photo collages, celebrating past events, community programs.

Kids, simultaneously street tough and wholesome, who had been through this kind of hell or that, redeemable or not, victims of circumstance or young sociopaths, smiling, hamming it up, eating corn on the cob, ribs, hanging in group homes, in church vans, riding horses, playing softball, clustered in group shots, wearing red shirts stenciled North Main Realty & Insurance, caps embroidered with a religious cross. In this last shot, girls gathered around a woman, early thirties; high cheeks, black eyes, hoop rings under dark hair, spiked white, pulled back but worn loosely. The eyes struck me, and the mottled complexion.

Her fans had scrawled on the photo.

Yeah, North Side!

We love you Dorothy!!

Champs!

I snapped a duplicate on my phone, then heard a door in the adjoining hall, heels clicking on the linoleum. A woman turned the corner: a big woman, brightly dressed, hair in dreads. She motioned past the sawhorses to the unfinished work, a half-dozen ceiling tiles removed and overhead ducts exposed. "You with County Health?"

"No."

"That's a city issue. They own the building. No budget for abatement. So, they tell us everything's fine, no problem, just so long as we leave it be. Then they send some fool from maintenance who tears down the tiles. Stirs a mess that don't need stirring."

"I'm not here about the asbestos."

"No?"

"Dorothy . . ." I gestured toward the photo of the young woman. "Dorothy Waters. She was close to a friend of mine. He died recently, and I thought she might want to know. His memorial service . . ."

It wasn't a lie exactly. It might have been true.

"We don't give out information on volunteers." She was polite enough, but I could see her hardening. "I'm sure you understand."

She stood with arms folded, the same treatment I'd gotten at the safe house. I was a type to her, someone to be wary of, a stranger looking for information on vulnerable women, on runaways and the people who tried to help them.

I went out the way I'd came.

▭

Outside, the gray sedan was gone.

I keyed the ignition, sat with the window down—waiting on that air-conditioner—meantime, comparing the photo I'd taken inside to the woman in the passport I'd lifted from Seeghurs' apartment.

The hair was different but it was the same dark glance, the same ragged complexion. The same woman, I was all but sure. Dorothy Waters, the guidance counselor, formerly known as Valerie Hite of New Mexico. Born again in the passport photo, aka Maggie Highsmith of Melbourne.

Three names, one woman. Three incarnations.

I'd been on the edge of that realization, back in that hotel room in New York. Now it came clear.

The neighborhood streets all funneled out the same way, onto a two lane, overparked feeder bounded by blind alleys and gravel drives, cyclone lots, vantage points from which an interloper might observe the traffic without being seen, then swing in from behind. I wasn't thinking about that possibility, though, and it wouldn't have mattered anyway. There was only the one way out.

I drove down the feeder to the old business district and parked across the street from Stev's Barbeque. Discolored brick, soot-stained windows—an older building that had survived urban renewal. I felt again what I'd felt earlier. The desire to go inside, to sit in the smokey room where Max had sat, across from his ghost. I could smell the brisket from the car. I should have followed that temptation, or at least checked the rearview. Instead, I compared the photos again, then wandered down the block to Akeesha Aimsley's office on North Main.

TWELVE

AKEESHA AIMSLEY WORKED as an insurance broker out of a single-story redbrick building along with her half-brother, who ran a real estate brokerage out of the adjoining office. Aimsley gave me the big smile when I walked in. She radiated a natural warmth, but at the same time her dark eyes sized me over.

"You aren't here to buy insurance," she said.

"No."

Her office seemed from another era: an old-fashioned oak desk, a large window, tinted, whose slatted blinds gave a view toward the street: cars crawling past, passersby moving slow on the sidewalk, small town slow, dead slow, heads bent, arms hanging loose, the storm continuing to gather, taking its time, distant, slow-rolling thunder. Amid that slowness, I saw the gray sedan pull to the curb across the street, the same man with the same dark glasses and straw fedora.

The consternation must have shown on my face.

"Is something the matter?"

"No," I said.

I showed her Seeghurs' picture and told her he was a colleague of mine who'd come to Omaha some time ago seeking background information for a story. "I am wondering if he stopped by."

"Why don't you ask him?"

Her skin was black, her lips full, a blossom of gray in the dark hair. She wore a necklace with a small cross, like the one worn by Dorothy Waters in the photo on the wall at New Hope.

"He passed," I said. "Of a sudden."

Sudden death is so common a euphemism for suicide that obit writers seldom use it any other way. My guess, Akeesha Aimsley—who served the church and worked insurance—would be likewise well-versed in the politesse of death.

"You have my sympathies," she said.

Her brother emerged from the other room. He was dark as his sister—a good-looking man in shirt sleeves, open at the collar, but without his sister's warmth, at least not toward me. He shook my hand, giving me that much, then stared pointedly at the street, at the shifting weather, the sudden darkening and the harsh light, at a teenage mother, belly big in front of her, moving slowly through the thick air. And at the man, too, the white man in the gray sedan.

"How did your partner die?" he asked.

Seeghurs hadn't been my partner, not for years, but I didn't argue the fact. The brother's office was steps away, within earshot. They'd shared the space for decades, according to Seeghurs notes. Meanwhile, outside, the man in the straw fedora glanced our way, to where we stood on this other side of the window, shadows behind the slatted blinds and tinted glass.

"I am trying to find someone." I turned back to his sister. "Dorothy Waters, I believe she worked with young women, in fellowship with your church . . . but she seems to have disappeared."

"Akeesha . . ." her brother interrupted.

She put up her hand, shook him off. She was older, the deacon at the church, the one who had known Dorothy. She glanced through the tinted glass to the man outside. He'd tailed me without my knowing, watching from the side streets.

"You should understand, a lot of women who work with troubled youth, they have their own histories. Then someone comes along, like your friend—a person of some reputation, a crusader . . ." She paused, giving me a look. "She might open up at first. She has a past to unburden. Wrongs to right. But old ghosts, they have a way of returning. Especially—you whisper their names. Your friend, of course, he had his own agenda."

She was right about that, but Dorothy Waters had had an agenda, too. Sources always did. Sure, maybe they felt the need to do the right thing—to erase some wrong—but it was rarely that simple.

"She visited Max in Brooklyn," I said. "But she left some things behind."

"What kind of things?"

"Identification, money."

I saw Akeesha Aimsley's concern. She knew something of her parishioner's old life, had taken her in. If the woman meant to start over . . . she was going to need those items.

"Has she been in touch?"

Akeesha didn't respond. She wasn't sure about me—and her brother, I could see, wanted me gone.

I nodded toward the man outside.

"That one, he's been in my footsteps."

The brother turned his upper lip. Neither he nor his sister spoke, and I fell quiet, too, not pushing. We watched the man smoke.

"Lost relative," Akeesha said at last. "That's what he says, but that's what they all say when they come poking around, trying to reclaim someone. Somebody who ran away—for goddamn good reason."

"Did he show you a badge?"

"Pimp, pervert, undercover police. Badge doesn't mean much. They come around. Then come around again. Different face, but it's the same son of a bitch underneath."

"How long he's been around?"

"He visited us last week, before that, I don't know."

I struggled with the timeline. Sometime after Seeghurs's death, the man had shown up on these streets looking for the missing woman. Now he was tagging me.

The man in the straw fedora put out his cigarette, making a show of it. He raised his eyes as if he could see us behind the tint, knew damn well we were studying him. Then he climbed into his car and drove toward Stev's Barbecue. He slowed near my car, hovering, then took the corner at the end of the block. Akeesha gazed out at that street, the slatted light falling across her dark face. Her fingers grazed the cross on her necklace.

"We can't help you," the brother said. "Whatever's going on, we don't want in the middle."

Akeesha took my measure. She might talk more if her brother was not here, but that wasn't the case. She turned warily to the window. Uneasy, I wondered if the man were still out there. He'd been shadowing me all day—or longer, since my landing, I wondered—and I didn't necessarily want to run into him. So, I asked if there was a back way, and the brother took me to the rear door. The iron screen opened into a mudroom, an enclosed porch with a barred window looking up the alley toward Stev's, at the painted billboard fading on its old brick. "Stev's in all the books," the brother said. "Tourists, whites from the other side of town. People like you, they go there all the time. No one kills them." He spoke the last as if it were regrettable.

"Go in their back entrance, then out the front. That way, if your buddy . . ."

"He's not my buddy."

"Go in the back, out the front," he repeated. "That way, if he's watching up the street, so far as he knows, you've been there the whole time. Better for us, better for you."

The man went inside to his sister.

I left the mudroom. I was cautious leaving, though not cautious as I should have been. I didn't glance over my shoulder to check the alley behind me. Then I heard a man clear his throat and I took that glance. The gray sedan stood in the mouth of the alley a few doors down. The man leaned against the wall in a spot where he could monitor the street and the alley both at once. He had circled the block, repositioning himself. I played like his presence was nothing to me and went on toward Stev's. He called out, and I heard him hustling over the gravel. I was inclined to run, but he might be a cop, and cops were inclined to shoot people who ran. I wasn't black but it was a black neighborhood, and I supposed he could say he'd gotten confused.

"Any luck?" he asked.

"I don't understand."

"Dorothy Waters—where she is? You have some information —these good people tell you something, it would be a wise idea to pass that along."

He regarded me with disdain. Dorothy Waters was his turf. He'd been looking for her before I showed. And been on me so quick, I wondered how he knew I'd been in town.

Accident, maybe, stumbling fate.

Or he'd been cued.

"Who do you work for?"

He didn't like the question.

"Your best play, stop looking. Disappear. Go back to your happy life, your dicking around."

I cut a glance at his car, at the plates. Those could be traced, if I caught the number, but he wasn't having it. He pushed his face into mine.

"You're a jackass," he said. "So I'll make it simple. You have two choices here." He held up his hand in demonstration, one finger, then another. "Get lost. Or get lost. That's it, Mr. Donkey. No carrots, no ears of corn. No tickle behind the ears. Just the stick. Or the stick. That's all we got."

He laughed, showing his teeth, big teeth, like a barnyard animal.

I repeated my question.

"Who are you working for?"

I should have known better, but I asked it anyway. Because I thought myself immune. In my profession, I'd grown used to a different milieu, people who operated more discretely. Or because I'd seen the widening smirk, and smelled the inevitable, and knew it didn't matter. He had a message to deliver and was going to deliver it.

I raised my head—trying to bluff, glancing to the plates again —but he grabbed me by the shirt front. I yanked away, back toward the wall. Trapping myself. He stepped forward.

"I can see you're confused."

He hit me then, in the stomach, the boxer punch straight to the gut. I bent over, gasping. It felt like my gut had split. My hand fell toward my pocket. The old gesture, not quite conscious. Reaching for the weapon that wasn't there. He grabbed my hand, spreading me open, and drove his right fist up into my chin.

My head hit the brick and I fell to the ground.

I must have lain for a while because the sky had changed color by the time I opened my eyes. I could hear a television and a couple in an apartment overhead arguing.

The car was gone.

Everything blurred. I stumbled into the restaurant. Entering not from the alley but the street side. The table help looked me over, so did the customers. I leaned against the counter near the register, pictures of old smokehouses yellowing nearby.

My shirt was torn, my nose bloody. The counter woman made no remark. I didn't want anything but ordered anyway. I needed to sit.

"I'd like some brisket," I said.

"Sides?"

"Whatever you think best."

The walls were covered with photos, stained from smoke, old photos, going back decades, the original Stev's, an outdoor barbecue, a pit out in the prairie, buffalo on a spit, a bluff somewhere, Indians gathered around an outdoor smoker. According to the table placard, Stev was the descendent of slaves, part Cherokee, who'd picked up his trade in the service while stationed in Texas.

A message from Anna appeared on my phone. We traded texts.

Where are you?

Omaha.

I'm stranded in O'Hare. You should go on without me.

I started to weep. I don't know why. Because I didn't want to be left alone in Omaha. Because something was loose in my head. Because I had a premonition. Because time had shuffled, and I wasn't in Stev's anymore—listening to the whispers from the next booth over—but further on, past the point of no return.

Here in La Bahia, my hotel room, the endless heat. Footsteps hissing down the hall. I wasn't going to make it home, to my beautiful life, not this time. I still held the phone. Time shifted back and Akeesha Aimsley walked in the front door.

"He beat you," she said.

"In the alley."

Sympathy troubled her face, but there was something else, too.

"I saw you stumble out."

"I'm okay."

I wasn't okay but said it anyway. She took a piece of paper out of a little pocket at the front of her skirt. Regarded me warily, as if having second thoughts. I regarded her warily as well and felt likewise leery of this slip of paper.

An address, a rural route. Somewhere in New Mexico.

"Why are you giving me this?"

"They had a deal. He was supposed to meet her here, in Omaha—but her old life . . . it was closing in. She couldn't wait. So, she gave me this—to pass on. In person, if he showed up here. Or called. But it was a one-way street. His number, she couldn't call. "

She looked at me, seemingly for an explanation. Seeghurs' cautions with his cell, especially toward the end, the paranoia, had made the mechanisms for contacting him more elaborate— burners, ever-changing numbers—but the reasons for the diffi- culty in this instance were likely more straightforward. He'd already been dead.

"What kind of deal?"

She shook her head. Between a reporter and a source, both parties might pretend otherwise, but everything was transac- tional. The missing woman had something Max wanted. And the other way around.

Information, something tangible. In exchange for safety, passage out. Money, a new identity.

"You didn't answer my question."

I saw the doubt in her eyes, wondering if she'd made a mistake trusting me. She wanted to help the missing woman, or just wanted that paper out of her hand. Me taking it the alley, the beating, had prompted her to go with her gut—sympathy, mixed with concern for her friend, the desire to do the right thing—but she had misgivings. Fearful not just for the lost woman, but the other people in her world. Her brother. Herself. I tapped the address.

"Is she here?"

There was a noise at the door. We both looked. Just another customer, no one that mattered—but she stood up to leave.

"I don't know," she said. "Go away. Leave us be. Help her if you can. Daughter of the Lord, children, all of us . . ." She shook a little then, weakening. "Just remember: that bit of paper, you didn't get it from me."

THIRTEEN

THE SKY WAS ragged. Behind me, in the rearview, the thunder anvils rose over the airport. There'd been a tornado the night before, wreaking havoc along the interstate, and the warnings were out again—but I'd had enough of Omaha. I drove ahead of the storm. Miscoulga seemed an eternity away but was not so far: on an island in the Platte River outside Lincoln, farmland gone fallow, purchased decades back by the Catholic Church. The old farmhouse, a monastery now, home for aging priests, stood dimly on the high ground above the Miscoulga retreat. The diocese had plans for the property, but the lower part of the island, below the bluff—a nest of old buildings just above the flood plain— remained under the control of the dying order, which leased it to the colony.

The storm let loose as I arrived, swamping the road to the main building. I stayed in the car. The fifty yards to the main house swelled in the storm. The cottonwoods shook and the rain ran in wide rivulets through the gravel, the sky and the ground and the water all blurring together, the lightning not outside but within, a seizure, a sudden crack to the skull. My gut hurt. I tilted my head back against the car seat. When the storm ended, the caretaker led me to my room, not in the main house but below: in the end unit of what had once been a bunkhouse for seasonal workers. I resisted sleep—worried, because of the blow to my head, but drifted off anyway. After midnight, a couple of cars rolled in, late-nighters from the airport, judging from the chatter, the wheeling of luggage across the wet gravel.

Are you awake?

It was Anna. The sound of the frogs rose and fell, tree frogs chirping, raising a high whoop, but bullfrogs, too, all kinds of croaking and twittering once you tuned in, so you could hear the mosquitos, a swelling hum, and the bats, or at least imagine them, their knife-edged flutter swooping from the eaves.

Yes, I'm here.

They have me in the Main Building.

Miscoulga had gone through several incarnations over the years. Aside from Main and the Bunkhouse, a dozen cottages lay scattered along the rise farther out, away from scrutiny. I'd been in one of those the year before, and Anna had been nearby. Cell coverage was sporadic—I'd tried Renée earlier—but seemed to be working now.

I brought his ashes.

For the service?

At first, I thought the Hudson. Or somewhere in NY. But he was fond of this place.

I get it.

I don't, there are too many bugs. Where do they have you?

The Bunkhouse.

I looked through the rear screen to the main house. People sometimes met on the porch steps. They talked quietly or maybe walked down the path. Places like this—away from one's usual life—things happened. Maybe those things meant something, maybe they didn't: a late-night walk, alone, a shadow almost visible, a white blouse, luminous on the path, then vanishing, nothing really, just the moon out from behind a cloud.

FOURTEEN

▭

THE MOURNERS GATHERED at the Main House, milling in the heat, then headed up the path toward a chapel on the bluff. It was midday, the sun still rising: no clouds, not yet, just the bugs and the heat and the humidity. I hung back, watching Anna in her thin blouse and skirt. She paused at the entrance, and I put my cheek against hers. People watched. Some in attendance had seen us together last year. She clasped my shirt, let me go. Seeghurs had been estranged from just about everyone by the time he died, but there were people who remembered him fondly. Some had made the trip, a few locals from Lincoln, scattered readers, admirers within driving distance, including a handful of old friends and colleagues: a reporter who'd worked with him at *The Tribune*; an organic farmer he'd profiled in a book condemning Monsanto; a woman who'd acted as his assistant before Anna came along, married now. Anna had been mentioned in *The Times* obit. People strained to get a glimpse.

The service struggled toward tenderness, reminiscence mixed with grief, an enhanced awareness—however fleeting—of the fragility of the moment, all these uplifted faces, people sweating in the heat.

Eventually, it was my turn to take the podium.

"I made some notes here on what to say, but decided not to use them, because, mostly, they're not true."

No one laughed, except for the guy from *The Tribune*.

"The last time I saw Max, it was here at Miscoulga," I said. "He and Anna. I hadn't seen him for years, but it took only an instant for all those years to vanish."

Anna's eyes met mine. I could see the sheen on her brow, her long neck, pale and white, her black hair, tied up but still unruly, face uplifted, the small flowers on her sheer, dark blouse. My head hurt from the incident in the alley, and my jaw was swollen. I glanced at Anna again and felt something falter inside. A line of strangers peered at me from along the back wall, sweltering in the crowded chapel. I told the mourners about my attempt to visit Max in Coney Island, then the conversation we'd had here in Miscoulga a year back. (I'd written this kind of thing for clients.) "Many ways," I said. "That conversation still goes on in my imagination. The kind of late-night talk I am sure many of you have shared here in Miscoulga. Where we discuss that difficult voice we struggle with, each of us, inside our own heads. Our vision, you might call it. The difference between what one wants to be true—what one needs to be true—as compared to that which exists."

What had happened that night—the last time I'd seen Max, still alive, here in Miscoulga, the year before—we'd been drinking, rye, like the old days. Anna eyed us from an old armchair whose piping had started to fray. She watched us, uneasy, legs crossed. To fill the space, I'd begun to talk California politics, a pulse

Seeghurs followed, though there came a point—regarding the Gaddis campaign (as yet undeclared)—where I'd had to play dumb. Seeghurs saw through that.

Don't you ever get tired of playing the shill? Of repeating their goddam lies?

It's not all lies.

It never is.

I could have come back at him. He'd botched things, like every reporter, suckered by what he wanted to believe, what he hoped to be true. I might have done so if not for Anna. She walked out to the porch, through the screen door. Seeghurs took the conversation back in time to that young woman, the forgotten intern at Cole & Clark, found dead in the Sacramento mud.

You should have left her alone.

You were the one who was sleeping with her.

I told you to stay away. She was mine. My source. But you . . .

We'd been through this years ago in the newsroom. The reality of it . . . his fault, mine . . . our mutual vanity . . . or the fault of the woman herself . . . naïve, foolish, thinking she'd get better protection inside the DA's office.

Also, your friend Jim Gaddis, golden boy in his expensive clothes, perfectly rumpled . . . Mr. High Cheekbones—with his baby blues . . . where do you think his money comes from, his stakes in those buildings, his contributors . . . the bright moral line, he's crossed it plenty.

I pushed through the screen door. Seeghurs grew more insistent, untethered. I understood his suspicion. *Your man, he's no innocent.* I'd felt it in my gut years before at that fundraiser for Gaddis in a luxury condo overlooking the American River. I'd leaned over the balcony, contemplating the restored riverscape, a promenade that retained, as architectural detail, planks from the old pier, the rotting dock onto which the coroner had hoisted the young woman's corpse. Behind me intermingled real estate developers, lawyers, off-shore clients who purchased the high-end units—also boutiques, shops, restaurants—the fruition of a reclamation project in which Mikel Rolland's Sundial had had an incipient role.

A little drunk, high, woozy on my proximity to these movers, shakers, I'd imagined connections underneath—they weren't hard to imagine (Gaddis had familiars in Justice, overseers, a stake in the development), though connecting the dots was a long leap, and how they connected, what story emerged, was better left sleeping in my imagination.

The bright moral line wasn't necessarily so bright as all that.

Anna went down the path, into the shadows.

Sundial, you can help me . . . you're an insider, and . . . I leaned my hand on the wooden porch post, hesitated. Then glanced back at my friend, disheveled, falling apart. *Of course you're not going to do that, you have too much skin in the game.* He paused, jutted his chin toward the empty path. *But the least you could do is stay away from her.*

▭

I swayed at the podium.

Max . . .

Lost my place, fell off-script. Searched for Anna's face in the chapel.

The audience stilled, fettering in the heat. I bowed my head, letting the silence take over, the heat soak through.

Whatever I'd prepared . . . whatever battered aphorism . . . lost in my notes . . . gone from memory.

I might have stepped away, but I'd waited too long, drawn attention to myself with the silence.

As if there were one last thing.

"Max was relentless . . . His pursuit of the truth . . . He didn't always find it—and what he did find, even if it exposed himself, his loved ones . . . He kept looking. There aren't many people who will do that, have that kind of love for . . . even if. . ."

The moment went ragged.

I shrugged.

Unable to finish.

But it was all right, I told myself, inevitable. The crowd teared. There was relief in that failure. Maybe people expected it, wanted to see it, even if the inexpressible was no comfort. I stepped from the podium. Another person took my place. Later, we streamed outside. We made a procession, under the midday sun and the towering cumulus, and moved along the rising path, through the stubbled meadow and the dragonflies and the humidity. We gathered on the hillock behind Anna and watched her scatter Max's ashes from the muddy bluff down into the Platte.

FIFTEEN

THE RECEPTION LASTED into the evening. I touched Anna on the shoulder, and she followed me to a wooden table under the trees. The dusk drained away, and the crowd grew quieter, smaller. Those remaining gravitated to the porch.

"I should get back soon. People might talk."

"They will anyway."

"I just came to get a cigarette."

I shook the pack. It was empty. "I have more inside."

The bunkhouse was primitive, but the studio had its charm: casement windows, tin lamps, a Luna moth stuck to the screen. The chatter from the porch filtered down. Anna sat gingerly on the edge of the bed, cigarette between her fingers, unlit. She'd been drinking, and her hair had come unleashed.

"What happened to you?"

She touched my cheek, then took me by the chin, turning me toward her, examining my nose, my swollen jaw, the gash at the back of my head.

"I tripped. Behind Stev's Barbecue—up in Omaha."

"What were you doing up there?"

"Waiting for you," I said, but that was only half true. "Also, for Dorothy Waters. That woman—who came out to Brooklyn before he died."

She glanced away.

The porch sounds lulled, faded to a murmur, broken by a woman's laugh, a soft laugh, sad, all but erotic in its bereavement.

"I need to go back up. His friends, some of those people, they came a long way."

"What did you know about her?"

"You're doing something for *Harper's?*" Anna's voice carried some trepidation. It wasn't *Harper's,* but it didn't matter. Word got around, accurate or otherwise. "At the memorial, you mentioned you were out to Max's before he died. You didn't tell me that."

"I tried to call. I took the subway out to your place."

Things had gone on between us longer than either of us had expected, then reached the point where either you walked out for good or didn't walk at all. Either way, everything changed. There was a widening rift, a giant chasm: a gap into which you fell, between this life and that, and in that gap, there was just this moment, then another moment. Who you were, in the stream of moments, was no one in particular. It was the natural state of human existence, one might argue, no matter how many identities you inhabited, or created for others, or shed to become someone new. I felt myself there now, in that gap, that empty space—but at the same time felt everything I had been, all my selves, clinging to me. Then, if only for an instant, this moment became luminous, Anna in the center of it, hands over her knees, still holding the unlit cigarette.

"You never broke it off with him all the way."

"Not quite."

"His manuscripts, his notebooks, they're still at your apartment?"

She shook her head.

"No. He came and got them earlier. The stuff he wanted . . . The rest I got rid of."

Their apartments had been rifled within days, if not hours of each other. Coincidence? Circumstances suggested otherwise.

A scrub operation.

To secure information, remove it from circulation. An old laptop—notepads, loose ends. People, too, apparently, if they knew too much.

"I've given myself another day here," I said. "Out to Tarkio Lake."

Anna knew the lake, an old fork of the Missouri left behind when the river changed course. She and I had gone out there the year before. My original plan had been to revisit Omaha the last day after the funeral. That didn't seem wise now, given the beating I'd taken in the alley. I'd tried changing flights, hoping to leave early, but between the spotty cell coverage and the storm delays I'd kept the original departure. The last I'd spoken to Renée had been on the tarmac in Denver, night before last. It seemed longer—but she knew how it was out here, the dropped calls, the bounced messages. Meanwhile, my return hadn't changed. I could spend my last day in Tarkio, and still be home as scheduled.

I'd already booked a room.

"Your magazine, what do you intend to say? That isn't your usual kind of work."

"I have done a lot of different kind of work."

She gazed at me with those gray eyes, then dropped her gaze to the ground: a familiar gesture, shyness, I'd thought at first. "I should go back—before people scatter."

"I'll walk with you partway."

The humidity persisted. I could feel my shirt dampening, the sweat pooling, and sense the warmth of her body under the thin blouse, the skirt. I caught the scent of her, mingled with everything else: the night smells, the dank, the fawn lilies and bloodroot. A line of trees stood between us and the voices on the porch. We stopped in the darkness beyond the light from the porch.

She leaned toward me in the darkness. I wondered if they could see us after all. I took her by the shoulders and hesitated, unable to see her features, to make out what was in her eyes. Something rose inside me.

The voices on the porch went silent.

She brushed her cheek against mine, and my hand touched her hips.

"I'm involved with someone."

"I know."

"How?"

"Your roommate told me. She also told me about the robbery."

Anna shrugged, but the gesture seemed too casual, too dismissive.

"What else did they take?"

"There wasn't much else. A little jewelry, some cash. Mostly they just scattered things around." Anna's voice trembled, though maybe it was just the long day, the emotion. "Regarding your article . . . There's something I should tell you."

"All right."

"It's kind of involved," she hesitated. "I need to say my goodbyes before everyone vanishes."

"Later, then."

"Tomorrow," she said." I can meet you at the lake."

I lay in bed listening to them on the porch, quiet voices

growing quieter, fewer in number. I wondered what she wanted to tell me—if she'd really show up at the lake. I took a shower before bed, but the night was warm, my sleep restless, the sheets sticky, and before long I was up again, running cool water over a rag.

SIXTEEN

Tarkio Lake was not really a lake but a remnant of the Big Tarkio River, an old tributary of the Missouri whose course had shifted and come to an end, pooling in the low hills some thirty miles past the state line. The old river ran shallow in front of the resort, just a roadside motel and a handful of cabins. A couple arrived shortly after me, birders who'd driven from St Louis, a harmless-seeming couple, talky, a little too much so, and I was glad when they headed with their cameras toward the thickets along the shore.

Anna arrived soon after. She wore a blue sundress. How she looked—emerging from her car, in her shades and her straw hat, swinging her white tote—reminded me of the summer before, when we'd followed the path along the lake.

"I'm on the late flight out," she said. "The red eye."

"Tonight?"

"After midnight. The drive's only a couple hours. So, I have some time."

"That's good."

"I brought my swimsuit."

She shrugged, a shrug I'd seen before, as if dismissing something that didn't want to be dismissed. Since Seeghurs' death, she'd spent more time traveling than in New York, nonprofit lobbying that took her to DC and various state legislatures along the Eastern corridor.

The birders roamed the edge of the thicket, facing away, taking pictures across the oxbow. The motel stood nearby, situated between the road and the lake: a line of rooms, each with a concrete stoop facing the shore. I'd already been to the office.

"What did you want to tell me?"

"I mentioned I'm in a relationship. Because of the situation, who he is, we've been keeping it on the down low, for now."

"Perry Lindemann."

She didn't seem surprised I knew the name: a sophomore congressman, out of Harrisburg, whose family had a place in Philly. Her roommate had let his occupation slip and I'd figured the rest. His was one of the districts her nonprofit had targeted, and he'd helped author a bill regarding water contamination from leaking waste containers.

"He's in a vulnerable position."

I saw where this was going: a married man, up for re-election, he couldn't risk his name linked to Anna's. It wouldn't do Anna any good either.

"Don't worry. I'm pretty skilled at these kinds of things."

"I'm not worried for myself."

"Why didn't you report the break-in?"

The birders came back out of the brush and settled at a table some hundred yards away. "They're darling," she said. Anna admired older couples. She wanted that someday, or what it appeared to be. I repeated my question.

"I told you, there wasn't much of value. Also, I thought it might be Max, at first." This didn't match what her roommate had told me, or what she herself had said the night before: that Max had already taken most his work, at her insistence, before the break-in.

"This woman, Dorothy Waters . . ."

Her reticence reminded me of that young intern. The dark hair, the clear eyes. The smell of her, the vulnerability, the ambition mixed with sudden fear.

"Dorothy Waters," I repeated. "AKA Valerie Hite . . ."

"I'd been keeping clear of his work—like I told you. I don't know anything about her."

She spoke a bit too coolly, chin up, reminding me again of the intern, an act, the sudden turn, her feigned offense at my inquiries.

I could push Anna but decided not to. It was hot. The birders were gone. A small bead of sweat gathered on her lip.

"I wouldn't mind going for a swim. Around the other side—where we went last year."

"It's a bit of a walk."

"What else are you doing?"

She was right. Max was beyond my reach, Dorothy Waters, too. The magazine piece, after my beating in Omaha—whatever ghosts I'd been trying to appease, whatever old self, lost in the tules of the Central Valley—I wasn't anxious to appease further. Likewise, Anna wasn't itching to get back to Queens. I stood up and she walked beside me. I'd taken the room here to avoid a return to Omaha. That's what I'd told myself. I opened the door to that room, let her in, then waited in the metal chair by the stoop. She came out wearing her suit under a white blouse. I saw her vulnerability, the fear in the wake of Seeghurs' death—of whatever she had gotten herself into with Lindemann, of that lonely apartment in Queens—and this all created a sense of inevitability. That and the feeling that whatever we did here, in the middle of nowhere, happened in a nothingness, and soon we would each disappear into that nothingness, down different jetways, but into that same empty space. Whatever we did, or didn't do, it ended in that emptiness—and maybe that's why we were both afraid.

"I don't think it was suicide."

"Stop," she said.

That was the crux of it, unspoken. Whispered at the funeral. My instinct—Max had not hung himself. It wasn't his nature. Also, the timeline, the chain of events: Whoever had strung him up, they'd scrubbed his apartment, and Anna's too. Then put the fedora after me. That's how it looked to me.

"They're not finished," I said. She glanced away. "You know more. Max talked to you, all the time. You typed his notes. The woman had something."

She tightened.

"Drop this," she said. What happened next, I suppose it was preordained. There was something raw between us, unfinished. We stood on the front porch in front of the motel door. She dropped her hands to her side, gave me a blunt look. "I might have stayed with Seeghurs if not for you."

"That's not true."

She shrugged.

"Maybe it was."

"You were done with him. You were just looking for somebody to help push in the knife."

Her eyes were ice now.

"Go home to your wife."

SEVENTEEN

▭

CALAMITY, NO MATTER how well foretold, has a way of blindsiding us. Later that day, I took a drive around the far side of Tarkio Lake, window down. The car's air conditioner had grown even more sickly. The air outside was hot, muggy. I was alone. After the scene at the cottage, Anna had driven off. I'd walked down to the river—looking for better reception, checking for messages from home, but it was as bad as Miscoulga. The storm must have taken down some local towers.

So, I drove the long circle, looking for reception. There wasn't any. The rear view was empty, and I told myself this was all over now, I could extricate myself easily enough. Forget about Max, the debris he'd left behind. Anna too.

A nameless fear rose in my gut.

The drive was longer than I expected. Near the end of the loop, I spotted a white hatchback on the gravel turnout adjacent to a darkening spur that wound to Stone Beach. Anna had been driving something similar, an indiscriminate compact of the sort airports rented in droves. I slowed down, pumping the brake—

but then let go. She'd wanted to swim in the lake out this way, but even if she had decided to, it was late and she'd be long gone, on her way to the airport.

Back at the motel, her blue sundress still hung in the closet. It meant nothing, she'd left angry, forgotten it. The car out at Stone Beach had no doubt belonged to someone else, evening hikers, maybe. I worried anyway. Natural enough, given all that had happened. I contemplated driving back to Stone Beach, but decided no. Maybe in the morning, on my way out of town—if the worry still tugged at me.

I imagined that as I fell asleep . . . again, later . . . now, these months later . . . the rippling water . . . the gray rocks on the shore . . . But I never made it out there.

Everything circles back.

Renée called in the morning, the signal restored. I was glad to hear her voice—though she quickly faltered.

"Your father . . ."

She starred to weep. I didn't get it at first. My mother had tried to get in touch the evening before.

My father had died of a stroke.

PART 5

DEPARTURE

EIGHTEEN

Home

THE SANTA ROSA Chapel stood not far from the hospital, on the fringes of a mid-century neighborhood, slab houses built on an old walnut orchard. Black walnuts, mostly, a variety that had proven less popular with people than with crows. Some of those trees were still around—in backyards, on street corners, on undeveloped parcels—and at the back of the mortuary lot. It was a large parking lot, empty except for the home's transport van and my sister's red Corolla.

It was hot here, too, a dead-feeling heat that smelled of the rural town Santa Rosa had once been, of those walnut trees, of the oak chaparral on those dry hills, with the turkey buzzards nesting above the drainage between Safeway and the nursing home.

Also, the smell of smoke. A grass fire at the edge of town, maybe. There was always a grass fire at the edge of town.

I found my mother, alone, in one of the mourning chambers,

a small room down the hall from the main chapel, curtained in dark velvet. She sat in a wingback chair, blind as ever. If she heard me enter, I couldn't tell. Because of her condition, she saw everything from the corner of her eyes.

"It's me."

"I know. You think I don't recognize my own son?"

I settled into the chair across from her. It was an intimate space, quiet, illuminated by a modest bit of stained glass. In some ways it was a relief to be here, away from that other life.

"Where's Liz?" I asked.

"In the crematory."

"Alone?"

"Your father's there. Your sister wanted to spend some time with him by herself. The undertaker took her back."

"It's not quite three."

"We got here early. Don't worry, the undertaker will be back for you. You'll get your turn."

"What about you?"

"No," my mother said.

My mother had been there when my father died. Unable to find the phone, lost in the sofa cushions, she'd sat with him for several hours until Mazie, their caretaker, showed up that evening. I thought it important she say a final good-bye, but my mother resisted the visitation. We would have a small service later, when his ashes were interred in the VA columbarium out at Memorial Cemetery.

"Are you sure you don't want to see him?"

"I only came for your sister, to keep her company. And for you. Me, I've already said my good-byes."

"You're sure?"

"I got my look." She'd been asleep when Mazie found them, his head in her lap. "So, I saw him. As much as I can see anything. Why do they keep those places so cold?"

I didn't disagree. The central air, a relief at first, cast a chill in the small room.

"It's worse than the grocery store."

"Your sweater?"

"I couldn't find it, and your sister wouldn't help. I'll drop dead from the heat, she tells me."

"There's your other sweater, you left in my car a while back."

"That black rag?"

She wore a rose-colored blouse. She disapproved of funerals in general and had made it clear, years in advance, she wouldn't wear black. So, she wore the rose-colored blouse she'd bought in Europe twenty-odd years ago. It was an elegant piece of fabric and looked good on her, and always had, maybe more so now that her hair had turned a brilliant white, gray mixed with platinum. Thicker than when she'd been a brunette, though it had been thick enough then. She didn't want to look like some stoop-backed peasant woman, all in black, trudging up a village street behind her husband's coffin.

"You look glamorous," I said. "Dad always loved that blouse on you."

She didn't acknowledge the compliment. She seldom did. Though she held her head up a little, lifting her chin.

"Your father was a sucker for glamour. His head, it was easily turned." Her manner reminded me of that time years ago—when my father had been working for the government, in the desert outside Los Cruces—and we'd seen him from the balcony of the apartment motel, down below us, outside the motel bar, idling with a young woman in a sleeveless dress, bright yellow.

"He wasn't really here, your father. It looked like he was here, but he was always somewhere else."

"That first stroke . . ."

"I'm not talking about the goddamn strokes. He was gone long before that."

"He spent a lot of time in his own head—in his work. But he loved you," I said. "And you traveled. You saw the world."

A dim light fell through the stained glass. It gave my mother the look of an aging woman in an old portrait, carefully rendered in failing light, the scaling paint and its darkening patina, still scaling, still darkening. "When he was a young, your father's vulnerability was plain to see. But he was talented. Those people he worked with, they were all arrogant bastards. They thought they were descendants of the gods." She pointed at the space in front of her, as if my father occupied it, a young man with broad shoulders and thick hair. "Out in the desert he told me he was channeling Oppenheimer. It made him feel powerful, but it was a torment for him, that son-of-a-bitch Oppenheimer inside his head."

Her eyes seemed focused on the image she had conjured, my father as Oppenheimer, an invention of the atomic mind. It was easy to forget how little she could see, how she glimpsed the world as if inside a closet, the door all but closed, the narrow slant of light growing narrower. "He wanted so much to be special, they took advantage of him. They hollowed him out. You must be careful," she said. "They'll do the same to you."

"I'm in a much different field."

"You keep their secrets," she said. "But I understand—for your family, for your career, it's better to play ignorant. Also, who doesn't enjoy power, hobnobbing? Your father . . . he never knew his own father, that snake in the grass . . . all the foster homes." I knew the story, how my father had grown up. My mother's voice changed, a touch of venom in her throat. "And his mother, Grandma Bobby, she was a real tramp."

The funeral director chose this moment to enter. A watchful woman in a blue suit. She held the door for my sister. If the woman had heard my mother, she gave no indication.

"I can take you back now."

She glanced from me to my mother, extending the invitation toward us both but in a voice that suggested—as she'd told me earlier over the phone, calmly, in a manner at once intimate and infinitely distant—people dealt with death differently, there was no wrong or right way about it. My sister settled into the chair next to my mother.

"We could have got him a nicer box."

"It's okay," my mother said. "I've seen him." She reached for my sister, touching her face with her fingertips, taking pleasure in the feel of her features. "I'll stay here with your sister, you go ahead."

The crematory was on the other side of the building, out back. I trailed the woman through the glass doors. The funeral director leaned into the heat, shoulders bent, a blonde-haired woman, tallish, pale. My mind was on the small things, the inconsequential ones. On the woman's flats. Her white legs. The asphalt that needed repaving. a pair of fence lizards in the open sun, puffing their throats before scuttering beneath the funeral van. On the crows too, peering down from the walnuts. I shadowed the woman into a small office leading to the crematory: a utilitarian chamber that housed the furnace and a man in a denim shirt, head bowed.

My father lay on a metal gurney, inside the strawboard casket: his name written in black marker on the foot of the box. The casket was open at the top, his face dusted with blush. He wore the clothes he'd died in. My sister had placed some sage in the box—for protection in the afterlife—and a few things he might enjoy. Old engineering books, a letter she'd written, family photos, a bag of chocolate kisses. Also, a small locket, trinitite and turquoise, a memento from White Sands where he'd worked for a while, near the nuclear ruins.

I had brought nothing. I crossed myself and closed my eyes, astonished at how blasphemous I'd become. I couldn't remember the prayers I'd been taught as a child, nor did I have the desire to remember. What came to me: how he'd comforted me, kneading my back with rubbing alcohol when I heard voices during a childhood fever. *Don't worry, we all hear voices.* I bowed my head deeper, touching my father's cold cheek with my own. *The time to worry is when the voices stop.*

The room was quiet except for the hum of the refrigeration unit from the storage chamber nearby. I looked to the attendant in his denim shirt.

"Okay," I said.

I helped the attendant wheel the gurney over to the furnace. He latched the handle and nodded toward the igniter button over its door: a red button, the size of my fist. I pushed hard, expecting resistance, but the button yielded easily. I heard the furnace ignite.

I followed the woman and her white legs outside into the heat, around the corner, back toward the main building. The transport van had left. The fence lizards were nowhere to be seen. More crows had gathered on the black walnuts and several of them squabbled over something at the edge of the asphalt. Then my mother and my sister emerged at the other end of the building, struggling in our direction, moving with some urgency. Before we converged, my mother pulled short, lurching over her walker, peering at our approaching shadows.

"She changed her mind," my sister said.

"Mom . . ."

"I want to see him."

No one spoke. We all just stood. Me and my sister and my mother and the undertaker, whose shoulders leaned into the heat. The silence communicated the essence of the matter. My mother blinked into the light. The woman leaned over farther and touched my mother on the shoulder.

"Oh," my mother said.

The undertaker continued down the walkway without us, dissolving into the glare. We headed toward my sister's car, moving along at a snail's pace, my mother nudging the walker over the asphalt, sweat pooling under her rose blouse. She shivered under the heat.

I helped her into my sister's Corolla.

"Give me my goddamn sweater," she said.

NINETEEN

▭

I RECEIVED A pair of messages that evening.

The first came from Gaddis (or one of his people, more accurately), wanting a meeting, on short notice, the day after tomorrow, an invitation for myself and Renée to an informal dinner at his place in the Woodlands.

Good news, on the face of it. An opportunity, at least.

A return to my old life.

I contemplated the dry hills from my office window. We had not been spared the heat, the temperature rising as the evening came on, the breeze no longer from the Pacific but from the interior, hot air spilling over from the Central Valley. The wind rushed along the ridges at the higher elevations, pushing the heat along with it, tumbling and sprawling over the Diablo Range.

I was still in my office, a bit later, when the second communication came, a text from an unknown number: no written message, just a photo: a man, his back to the camera, watching a woman approach. A woman in a blue sundress, swinging a white tote over her shoulder.

Myself . . . Anna . . .

I remembered the birders, the sweet older couple wandering with their cameras by the shore. The revelation shook me. They'd followed me, picked up where Mr. Fedora had left off. I'd been foolish not to see, too self-absorbed.

But why this? Why now?

Max had been tailed, too, all through his career. So he'd insisted. He'd been proud of it. *Bastard Feds, digging through my laundry. Spooks—psychological blackmail. Stalking the shadows. Trying to threaten me off the story.*

This might be that, or something similar. The idea wasn't reassuring.

Renée stepped into the room behind me. I put the phone, face down, on the window ledge.

"Are you alright?"

"I'm fine."

"Santa Rosa—I would have come."

"I know, but my mother . . ."

I left it there. She knew my mother. A dark-hearted woman, fierce, funny, who kept her grief in a box. If you weren't blood, that box stayed shut. Renée joined me at the window. "We're in for a heat wave. There's already fires up north."

A car rolled up our street, turned around in the wash at the end of the road. It sat there a while. Renée studied my face. I'd been followed not just in Omaha but out to Tarkio, too.

I wondered now about the car in the wash. It idled a little longer. Then went back the way it came.

▭

Before the meeting, the Gaddis campaign sent over the latest report from Hastings & Hastings, pages of polling and focus-group data accompanied by analysis, demographic breakdowns, positional strengths and weaknesses, hypothetical strategies, the kind of thing I'd read a hundred times, or pretended to. The essence was easy to determine. Gaddis's numbers were good, but there were underlying concerns. I understood the problem he faced. It wasn't his politics so much, or his positions on the issues, but the ineffable stuff. He exuded vanity, privilege. It wasn't altogether fair, a misperception of sorts, but still not to be ignored. A child of divorce, raised by his mother, he'd had a migratory adolescence, around the edges of affluence but not quite in it. As a high school kid, he'd worked (or so the story went) several jobs at once, struggling his way into college, a young man who might have slipped over the edge (and this was the other side of the story) if not for his good looks and a wealthy uncle who'd brought him into the family business. He was a little too attractive, a bit too pleased with himself, and because of his money, his beautiful wife, his celebrity, his youth (though that was rapidly fading), he tended to get under the skin of even his natural constituency. None of this mattered so much in the current race—given the state of the opposition—but it didn't bode well for the national stage.

▭

I had expected the meeting to be a mixer, but it was just Gaddis and his wife, Candice, together with Renée and me—and a cell minder who wandered in and out, at Gaddis's behest, with news on the wildfires. Calistoga was threatened, and several towns in Lake County had already burned. The smoke hadn't reached us yet, but it would.

"You need to be there," said Candice.

His wife had worked in television news, most recently as a producer for a documentary on the Macron campaign, notable for its unvarnished portrayal of the French citizenry, a paradox-ical portrait, both brutish and intelligent, that had helped Macron break through beyond his natural constituency. Renée had had passing interaction with Candice in the past, down at the embassy, so they knew each other. Candice had no official role in Gaddis's campaign, but I knew she'd conceived a whistle stop tour, The Big Blue Bus.

"Cinéma vérité," she said. "With a touch of the avant-garde."

"I don't know how that will fly in the Central Valley," said Gaddis.

"They're not your only audience."

"No, but they're the ones I need to reach."

The cell minder brought a tablet, and Gaddis scanned the news himself. "Evacuations have been ordered for Chico, too," he said. "Meanwhile Route 12 is closed. Lake County—people can't get out. They either get incinerated in their houses, or in their cars."

"You need to go up there," Candice repeated.

"That's the governor's call."

Gaddis leaned back, a rangy man, aware of his looks—eyes brimming—but with a sudden smile, boyish, almost shy, that conveyed a diffident charm. He grew earnest. "These kinds of moments, they aren't just ceremonial. They can't be scripted."

"It's a delicate balance," I said. Gaddis and his wife were strong personalities. I didn't want to get caught between—but I had, at some point, to speak. "Queen Elizabeth and the Welsh miners. That tragedy, she almost waited too long—not wanting to get in the way." I realized it might not be the best example, bringing up royalty. "Also, closer to home . . . Katrina . . . Sandy Hook . . .Times like this, when the raw human face reveals itself, that's when a leader needs to be there. The divisions, the us and them, the political divide. These kinds of moments, they have their own shape, unexpected revelations . . . about the values we share."

"That's true," said Gaddis.

Maybe it had been the right thing to say. Or close enough. The table grew more relaxed. Conversation turned toward the homeless, the decaying infrastructure, foreign trade. Renée joined in. She participated, showing her knowledge but not too much. She was aware of her role. The loyal wife, good, bright, with her own ambition, but savvy enough to keep out of the way.

"I love this prosecco." Renée worked with the French, who disdained the stuff. Italian trash. In which vintage meant nothing. The nature of the grape, a year or three—it went bad in the bottle. "Yes," agreed Candice, "It's quite delightful." Though one suspected—as Candice raised her glass—that she might share the French attitude. But then again, well, not every occasion merited champagne. "To the moment," she said.

After dinner, Gaddis took me down to his study.

"I've tried these last months to articulate a vision. Something more than one can get across in ten-second sound bites. Or those internet grabs."

"Your position papers . . ."

We'd gone over this six months ago. I'd suggested that he take me on the Big Blue Bus. Give me a chance to capture his voice. Put out daily posts, sometimes about himself, his ideas, but giving equal measure to the people and places, the land swelling outside the windows, human observations that could serve as a building block for something longer range—a vision that didn't get caught in the fuss and details of policy. He'd stopped, mid-stride, in his jogging shorts when I'd said that. Offended by the observation, unspoken, that his policy papers were dry as dirt. He hadn't said anything but simply resumed running, building speed, leaving me behind.

I was in better shape now. The reason he'd come back to me, I guessed—his analytics, the people at Hastings told him he needed something more. Instead of revisiting our old conversation, I admired the books in his study, lingering by the political memoirs, the biographies, the letters and speeches: Grant and de Tocqueville, Obama and McCain. King. Caesar and Lincoln. The Roosevelts, Eleanor and Franklin both, Chavez, Ayn Rand...

"Which one is your favorite?"

An absurd question—there can be no favorite in books or ideas, unless your mind has been enclosed in a cocoon (as is, sooner or later, always the case)—but I asked it anyway. He pulled out *Profiles in Courage*.

"Ah, Sorensen," I said.

"No. JFK."

By his smile, I could see he knew otherwise. Yes, it was Kennedy's name on the cover. Yes, the book had won the Pulitzer and helped Kennedy win the election. But the writer— who had sat alone with the material, after all the talk was over, after Bobby and Jack had gone to bed, after the whiskey had been drunk and the campaign hall emptied—was Ted Sorensen. Sorensen had been Kennedy's speechwriter. Gaddis knew that, too, no doubt, but I didn't press the matter.

"Kennedy was the visionary," I agreed.

"It's not about one person." Gaddis gave me his smile, the same one he'd given Renée in the opera box, and I felt his charm pierce through.

"I heard about Max Seeghurs passing." He put his hand on my shoulder, a moment of warmth, empathy. "I know you two were close. Hard-nosed reporter, seeker of the truth."

"Yes."

"We could use more like him."

"Yes," I said again, though I knew the admiration, even if

sincere, had not gone both ways. Max had not cared for Gaddis, a native dislike, from the gut—and wanted to take him down. Likely Gaddis knew that.

But I'd seen Max's notes. He had no substance on Gaddis, just suspicion.

"He had habit of chasing phantoms," I said.

"Don't we all."

At Gaddis's direction I got in touch with Eileen Watson, his chief press deputy. Campaign subordinates, their names and identities, all tended to blur after a while, but Eileen Watson was higher up. She had a reputation as a press whisperer—someone who fed leaks to the media, advance stories, and had done a fair amount of hatchet work in the past.

"Jim asked me to give you a call," I said.

Watson enjoyed the hard-knuckled stuff. She'd worked with a Republican governor, and on the Dole campaign, but had switched sides to work with Gaddis. She liked a winner. Then she brought up Angela Morales, the party's senatorial candidate, just as the earlier handler had done.

Angela's race had been heating up, drawing attention.

"The party supports her, as do we. But that race, the closer it gets, the more brutish. We just don't want to get caught by surprise—if there's something in her closet . . . that might tarnish that star of hers. We don't want to be too close, you know how mud splatters . . . up and down the ticket."

"I do," I said, though I suspected this had little to do with protecting the party slate. Watkins knew I'd worked for the legislator who'd help launch Morales. Part of my job had to been to seek out the unpleasant details on his protégés.

"I know Gaddis is drawn to working with you." Her voice

carried the sound of an old news house, no nonsense, keys clattering and phones ringing upstairs, web press clanking in the basement, newsprint pressed onto paper cranked through giant rollers. "Before we bring you on, we need to know your loyalty is with us—not to some pissant non-disclosure you signed with her mentor two decades ago. Whatever you know about Morales, we need to know, too."

Technically speaking, what she was asking, it was unethical—but that didn't mean it never happened. Candidates were always collecting intel, leverage, even on people in their own parties. Especially so, as those rivalries could be the fiercest.

The enemy within. One had to be prepared . . . primaries down the line . . . two years, four . . . when they were competing for the larger prize.

"And no freelancing. Not with *Esquire, The New Yorker, Politico,* anyone at all, any topic. Nothing that hasn't been vetted by the campaign." This wasn't unusual, but I remembered Gaddis's hand on my shoulder and suspected what lay underneath. It wasn't just intel on Morales they wanted. The campaign had found out about my article on Max—the one Fred had arranged—and wanted it shut down. I might have objected, but that story was a minefield. Also, I had other considerations, more practical.

"I'll need a retainer."

TWENTY

RENÉE CAME HOME late, after a long day with Robert Lille, an embassy client hoping to attract some biotech companies to northern France. There'd been a rash of these lately, with similar objectives, all but interchangeable. Lille spoke English well enough but needed help on some of the nuances—especially in regard to the jargon. More than that, he wanted to be shown around, to have someone accompany him. He liked to have a woman with him at the table when he discussed business— someone whose ear he could lean into and whisper.

"There's only so much of that I can take."

Renée enjoyed disparaging him: he smelled of deceit, of escargot, of those urinals hanging on lampposts on Parisian streets. Part of me suspected something else lay beneath the pleasure she took.

"You disparage him too much."

"He enjoys it."

I watched her undress.

"You arranged things with Gaddis?"

"Almost."

The heat was also too much, inside the house and out. Too hot to think, too hot to sleep.

"What do you want to do?"

"We could fuck." She said it dryly, serious or not, I couldn't tell. It sounded like something Lille might say, only in French. *Mets da zob dans mon cul.*

"All right."

"In a little while—when it cools down."

She drew on her silk robe, and we went down to the pool, where the kids lay sprawled like exhausted cats. Renée hung her feet into the water and expressed again her dislike of the Frenchman.

"He's charming. He knows how to dress, how to flatter, to give you long looks like he's listening. But it's too much, it's exhausting. Also . . ." She let it hang long enough to catch my imagination. "He's a liar. He told me his parents were in the resistance—with de Gaulle. He told me he met Camus."

"They all say that."

"He was too young to have met Camus. Or else he's lying about his age. Also, his father sold medical supplies to the Germans. And later to the Americans. They played every side."

"Maybe they had no choice."

"They all say that, too."

The pool was too warm. According to the weather report, the heat was supposed to have broken already, the wind shifting, but that hadn't happened. The air smelled of smoke. "Why don't we go inside. Maybe it's nicer in there."

"It isn't."

"You can make me a drink."

We went inside together, lingering over the ice in the sub-zero. We kissed with the freezer door open.

"We could go to a movie theater. They have air conditioning at least."

"Why don't you fuck me instead."

We put ice in a bucket, sucked on the chips.

I touched her between the legs. She was warm there, and damp, and put her long tongue in my ear, cool from the ice.

We went upstairs.

She undid her robe and lay on the sheets under the fan.

"It's still too hot."

We reached across the bed, fingertips touching. The heat did not break, not till later, after we had worn ourselves out resisting —first with vodka and ice, in front of the fan, then in the bed itself, under the thin sheets—a perverse, sultry resistance, rubbing against each other in the dark, taking refuge in the flesh, damp with sweat, a fierceness that ended with my head buried in the wet linen, skin titillating under the sheen of perspiration. It was still miserable, lying there, mouth open, drooling onto the bedclothes, a misery like a childhood fever—after it had gotten so bad that nothing else existed, and relief was a pale ghost growing paler, until finally the ghost passed, a convulsive chill, and the fever broke.

I woke earlier than Renée, before dawn. The temperature had dropped. I lay looking at her, and for an instant nothing else existed, just Renée, the ashen curl on her neck, her breasts exposed, her fingers intertwined in the sheet. She was hard into sleep—away from everything, lost in the moment—the balmy wind, the dirty pillows—and I felt as if we had returned to our natural state.

Then I heard my phone vibrate.

I felt the chill again, the ghost passing through. I told myself it might be Santa Rosa. Or Gaddis. A Nixle alert from the county sheriff. A coupon from some retailer. I closed my eyes and edged toward Renée.

The phone shook another time, vibrating on my nightstand.

The texts were anonymous, like the earlier ones, from a number I didn't recognize.

Another picture of Anna. Of myself. Different angles this time. Standing in the doorway to the room at the motel.

I climbed out of bed and stood in the dawn light.

Renée lay as before.

The scent of her filled the room.

I figured I should delete the photos, but the images tugged at me. I know things aren't supposed to be this way, but my emotions aren't pure, they linger here and there, in places where they shouldn't. I hate people even if I love them. Great waves of devotion rise up inside me and fill me until I am a hollow drum. More pictures came, close shots, long, showing a quarrel on the porch.

The reason these were being sent to me? An implicit threat ... to expose the affair . . . blackmail, maybe, or just harassment ... of the sort Max had talked about, Though the end game, in my case . . . I was about to hit delete when the phone vibrated once more.

Renée rolled deeper into her sleep.

I stepped out of the room.

The text contained a link to a news story about a New York woman whose body had been found at the bottom of a ravine not far from Stone Beach.

One Anna Gilbert, 37, of Queens.

Max's Anna. Mine, too.

Her photo, taken from her driver's license, accompanied the text. Likewise, a shot of her rental hatch car on the road above.

Anna was dead.

The realization was a cold one. I saw myself from a distance, a thin shadow tilting over his cell phone in the emptiness at the end of the hall.

The shadow had an ache in his chest.

I'd felt this coming, out at the lake, but was blindsided anyway. Her death, no accident, I thought, no random tumble. She'd known more than she'd admitted. Maybe not so much in the greater scheme of things, but too much. Seeghurs' confidante, with his journals in her home, or what remained of them, scribblings, a busted laptop, all gone now too, scattered and seized.

Never mind what she'd forgotten or thrown away.

Police were investigating, canvassing the locals—to see if anyone had seen her beforehand, or could explain what she had been doing in the area, or who she might have been with.

TWENTY-ONE

▭

THE SEDAN PASSED me and pulled into the gravel wash at the end of the street. Two men got out: the passenger first, in a grey suit—pausing deliberately behind the open car door, a shield of sorts—and then the driver.

My daughter scampered farther on, already up the hill.

"Mr. Reynolds?"

The man on the passenger side hung back, tall, thin, almost dapper in his gray suit, one hand tucked discreetly into his jacket. It was the other man who spoke my name, the thick-chested one in shirt sleeves. He slid toward me over the gravel.

Renée had left for work, and Lena sought a fresh supply of milkweed for her monarchs in the breeding cage. She'd been feeding them milkweed raised in our garden, but it turned out to be a tropical variety, carrying parasites that ate the caterpillars from the inside, leaving black smears in the cage.

The man in the shirt sleeves showed me his identification.

"Agent Moore," he said. "FBI."

The tall man in gray showed me nothing. I'd learned from an

earlier client that agency boundaries were not always as firm as one imagined: federal mixed with local with state with Homeland Security with immigration with corporate hirelings with the criminal underground. Sometimes it was well coordinated, but often as not there was a mess underneath. Also, the ID cards were an easy bluff. When confronted, people didn't always look as closely as they might, or know what to look for.

"We'd liked to ask a few questions. Concerning a friend of yours—Max Seeghurs."

I caught a glimpse of Lena up the hill, on an exposed bit of trail where the path spurred around the ridge.

"And his wife," the other added.

He spoke from farther away, the other side of the car, an edge in this voice, a fleeting smile, his face brimmed in shadow.

"My daughter. You probably saw her pass."

"You're a family man."

His voice held that same edge, and that same fleeting smile creased his face. I addressed the other one, Agent Moore. I knew Seeghurs had run into trouble for violating national security protocols in an earlier investigation (focusing on a corruption scandal he couldn't prove, involving the House Intelligence Committee, backdoor relationships, payouts). I also knew—because that Brooklyn cop had told me, in that late night call—that the Bureau had been looking into his death. Not necessarily out of fondness for him, or sorrow over his demise. He had a habit of pushing places they didn't want him to go.

"She'll get worried if I don't show up, and I'm not comfortable her wandering alone."

Moore's face was unreadable.

"*Your* identification?" he asked.

Technically, I didn't have to talk to them on the spot, just like they couldn't arrest me without a warrant.

I handed it over.

"My daughter," I repeated.

Moore shot a look at his gangling partner. The man twitched, an indecipherable shrug, and I wondered about the hierarchy between them.

"Alright," Moore nodded. "Just don't get lost up there."

"We'll be waiting," said the other. He twitched again, less ambiguously, as if hoping I'd be fool enough to bolt.

▭

Lena wandered with an eye for trails that snaked into the thickets, and she wandered those thickets into deeper thickets that opened suddenly onto unexpected meadows. As a child, she'd been fascinated with the small stuff, but unlike other children in our neighborhood, who learned to hurry along as they grew older, her destination remained in the minutiae, the small creatures who lived under the rocks: the Jerusalem crickets, the ants, the beetles, the black bugs, the insect larvae. She could identify the plants, the larvae under the leaves. Up here, in these hills, there existed two varieties of milkweed. The one she needed thrived in disturbed ground, at the edge of paths, along rights-of-way and easements, under electrical wires, atop cable trenches.

I huffed my way toward her.

"What was that about?"

"What?"

"Those men . . ."

"A work thing."

"Their car's still down there."

"We have an appointment."

"Shouldn't you go?"

"They can wait."

The tall thin man in the gray suit leaned against the car, but

Moore had vanished. I'd seen him on the trail behind me, following at a distance—keeping an eye on me.

"Where's the milkweed?"

"We have to be careful."

"About what?"

"Some varieties harbor mites."

She tilted over a plant and studied it forever: a soft-eyed kid, glasses like giant windshields. We'd done this kind of thing plenty of times. She kept on peering, absorbed, even after something scuttled in the brush behind us.

"Just a deer, dad." She didn't look up. "Or those wild turkeys. Dumber than dirt."

We climbed the crest to where the power lines ran along the ridge, then up an untended slope, ground cleared by a brush fire a few years back. A eucalyptus grove dominated the next ridge down. The fresh slope was her secret place, her treasure trove. The milkweed plants were small and bristly, the leaves narrow. She searched for plants the butterflies had visited, leaving their eggs on the underside; for caterpillars who had hatched; for hanging cocoons as yet undisturbed by the red-eyed flies who feasted on the pupa.

It was the usual mess, the whole chain of being, one creature consuming the next.

"Look," she said.

She'd found a string of pupas, where maybe a half dozen caterpillars had woven cocoons along a low-hanging branch. The chrysalis had turned black, quivery, about to burst, about to bloom, but something was not right. A small head crawled out. Then another.

"Wasps," she said.

Lena examined her field jar, its fat caterpillars, eggs glimmering on the underside of the green leaves. I heard twigs crunch and saw over her shoulder down the switchback to Agent

Moore, thick-chested in his shirtsleeves. He stood firm, wanting me to register his presence, before stepping back, fading into the madrone.

My daughter's eyes went wide.

"These others are healthy," she said, holding up the jar. "I think so, I hope. I'm pretty sure."

We walked down the path, toward the gangly man in the wash. Moore trailed behind. She chattered, nervously, in the way kids do. At once uncertain, precocious. Talking about nature, its disguises, how one thing transforms into another. Butterflies being the souls of the dead. According to the Indians, at least. Bright beams of lights, except of course if the mites get to them. Then they turn to something else. Not so pretty.

I took her the rest of the way home, then went back alone to join the men at the car.

TWENTY-TWO

▭

"WHERE ARE WE going?"

I had assumed we'd talk in the car, but Moore turned the ignition. The other one sat in the seat behind me.

"Field office."

I thought this meant the Civic Center, a dust-colored building dug into the hillside over the county jail, but Moore dropped under the freeway onto Francisco, a street of car dealerships and repair shops fronting the Canal District. He wheeled across traffic, down a side street, pulling into a motel identifiable as such only by its ugliness and an oversize sign.

Nightly Rates

Dayworkers lingered in front of Rafael Paints across the street, though not so many as before the immigration sweeps. Agent Moore and his tall friend prodded me along the outside stairs of the motel to the second floor. Up close, the man seemed even taller, oddly thin, gangly, disproportioned.

We went single file, me in the middle. If I made a fuss, all the cards were in their hands. They could push me over the railing or drown me in the dirty water of the canal, no one was going to do much of anything.

The dayworkers slipped away.

Inside, the furnishings had a secondhand look, frayed sunbursts fading on the carpet, décor inherited from a chain that had de-branded the building and moved to a fresher location closer to the off-ramp.

"Sit down."

Moore still wore the same mask of professional reasonableness, the good cop, but he wasn't armed, at least not visibly, which made me think he was a desk man—corporate fraud, forensics, paper investigation—who only made it to the field on occasion, and that the man with him, however gangly, was the muscle. Moore's smile was not a smile so much as a crack in his mask, and through that crack I saw a harder something underneath.

"What's this about?" I asked, friendly enough, matter of fact as I could manage, though I was thinking I'd made a mistake coming along like this, no lawyer, no outside contact, no reassurance these men were who they claimed.

"What do you think it's about?"

The tall one stood by the bed, no longer dapper, too tall for the room, even more gangly. The ceiling was low, and he was out of proportion to the room.

"Coney Island. Omaha," said Moore. "You've been traveling a fair amount."

"Occupational hazard," I said.

"Also, that little cottage in Missouri—across the state line."

"Tweet, tweet," said the other.

I got the joke. They'd seen the pictures. Courtesy of the birders, no doubt, who'd picked up my trail after the Omaha thug worked me over in the alley. Former agency man, I figured, something like that, disgraced cop, private mug, brought in to secure the missing woman. Scare me off the scent. Not particularly artful, though. Subtle as a brick.

Strong possibility, he didn't even know who hired him. A third-party arrangement.

Not exactly by the book, but everyone hired contractors now, including the Feds. It gave them wider range, plausible deniability.

The motel room held no suitcases, no evidence of inhabitation. Just a lumpy bed, a queen, and a phone on the bureau: a landline, old school, coil cord and push button.

"Why here?" I asked.

Moore had shown me his identification at the car. Now, as if to reassure me, he slid his business card across the table: the FBI emblem, the address of the San Francisco Office, his title: *SPECIAL AGENT, INTEGRATED MISSIONS.*

"Your side of the world, I suppose there are bigger budgets. Us, civil servants, things can get a bit austere. Our profession, to collect information. Very similar to your own. How information gets interpreted, what gets omitted or retained—that's the art of it, I'm sure you can appreciate."

Moore grew more affable, a lilt in his tone. He had a thick face, a wide nose, curly hair, Irish looks, though darker, Black Irish maybe, a little Carthage thrown in, from back when Rome paid its mercenaries to ravage the Celts. The tall one had a hawk nose and pale skin, Lebanese, Polack, Jew, gargoyle, it was hard to know. Another mongrel. Not unlike myself. Part this, part that, a mix of dust and water and chemical that took its colors from the pigment in the dirt.

In another world I might have had an affinity for these two, imagined something holy in their ugliness—the scent of human mixed with the goon—but in this world . . .

"Those were your people. The ones who tagged me . . . that fat fuck, who gave me the lump on the head?"

They said nothing.

The matter was immaterial. What fat fuck, what fedora? And as for the birders—aging snoops, their affiliation, inside the agency or out, mattered less than the photos themselves.

But those shots made me a person of interest in Anna's death.

Moore reached down. He pulled up a shoulder case, not unlike the case I carried on the job. He unsheathed his tablet and dialed up a picture of Seeghurs on its screen, taken after I'd last seen him, further decomposed—still hanging from that same bench in Coney Island.

"Max," I said, the name ushering itself out of me, low and sad, involuntary. The sound of my own grief took me aback. My feelings for Max were mixed, but he'd been a friend once upon a time, or something close, and you don't get many of those.

"The Brooklyn cops like suicide," Moore said. "But these ligatures, the way the cord bites the neck, that angle, suggests strangulation from behind. So, I like homicide. The scuffed clothes, bump on the head. Sure, maybe he got drunk, stumbled down the stairs, strung himself up. Or maybe he had some assistance . . ."

Moore waited a beat, giving me a chance to ponder. Seeghurs had made enemies over the years—in the corporate world, in government (within the intelligence apparatus, too). I wasn't sold on suicide either, but these two had their agenda.

"What was your relationship to Anna Seeghurs?" he asked.

He dialed another picture: Anna in the ravine—an unnatural angle: back arched, head blunt against the stone. Black hair, blood-cotted, unruly, spiraling up like some bush sprouting from the ravine.

"Stone Beach. Out by the lake. There's a path up above. But

the injuries, forensics says, the blow to the skull. Inconsistent with a fall. Lug wrench, more likely. Beaten first, then pushed. Also, a second set of footprints. Vikram soles, very common," he paused. "You might have some yourself."

I saw where this was going.

My illicit lover, her ex-husband. Both dead. Anna at Tarkio. Max in Brooklyn. Each incident, I'd been in the vicinity. They could build a case, all circumstantial—but people got convicted on less. I felt a panic in my heart. Even if the case never made it to trial, even without an arrest—just the insinuations. My marriage . . . my career . . .

The tall man had been quiet, sitting on the low queen, all angles, his long legs skewed, knees up high, elbows crossed. He leaned forward.

"We all make mistakes." His voice sounded as if might be coming from some distant place, through a speaker in his chest. "Then coincidence conspires, circumstance—a sudden flare of temper, who knows—and our little mistakes become big. One thing follows another. You fuck a man's wife. Or her blue dress. Maybe you fuck that . . ." I held my tongue. It was what you were supposed to do in situations like this. "One thing I don't under-stand. You're a hack—a mouthpiece." He spoke with disgust, eyes agleam, a smile that quavered, went away. "So, what are you doing playing reporter all over Omaha, looking for Dorothy Waters. aka Valerie Hite? Why? Even after you're back home, you keep it up. All that poking on the internet."

He smiled that smile again, letting it settle on me, sly, long enough to see I'd gotten the message: they'd been tracking my footsteps not just on the ground but in the digital world, too, warrant or no.

"Why?" he repeated.

"He's an idealist," said Moore. "Down underneath."

"His ideal is his dick."

The thin man shook his head as if he'd seen it before, whatever people pretended, however much they feigned, it got down to the same thing.

"I have to piss," he said.

He went into the bathroom. He pissed with the door open. Moore studied me, bemused. My glance fell to the table, to his card: *INTEGRATED MISSIONS*. I wondered what side of which agency boundary, within which departmental jurisdiction, this mission might fall, but also realized my situation, right now, these technicalities were irrelevant. It was me and them. The other one rattled around in the bathroom, water on, water off. He came back with a glass and a pint bottle.

"Drink?"

I shook my head.

There had been a similar bottle on Max's workbench in Coney Island, rye, half-empty. Suicide by hanging was hard to stage, I knew from my time on the beat. Strangulation from behind, sure, one man could handle that part. But lifting the guy, wrapping him to the bench, would require another pair of hands. Two men, working together. The gangly agent stepped to the dresser and dropped his hand on the landline, toying with the cord.

I glanced from one to the other.

"Seeghurs was looking into Sundial, the Bureau was aware of that," the man went on, "his book contract." He scoffed. "Also, he'd submitted information requests—DOJ, this, that—combing the probes—but he bogged down. Delusional son-of-a-bitch. You could see it in his notebooks, that scrambled manuscript. Half-finished, scattered all over his little dump in Coney," he paused, not realizing what he'd let slip, or not caring.

There'd been no manuscript by the time I got there, none of Max's usual disarray, no evidence of work in progress.

Someone had been there ahead of me.

These two. . .

"But Hite, what the fuck did he want with her?"

"I don't know."

The question struck me as a rhetorical, the kind cops pull during interrogations, when they have their own information and hold it close. Whatever Max had hoped to learn from the woman, whatever she possessed, these two knew better than me. I'd searched his notebook, the elaborate charts, my own memory. Lost myself in that fever dream, the tangle of names. There were too many gaps, missing nodes, lines that ran parallel, intersected, veered away . . . through different players . . . multiple organizations . . . culminating in projects on this coast or that . . . the heartland. Some distant murk.

Investigations like this were booby-trapped. Touch here, pry there, the spring came unsprung, the mechanism collapsed, and the inner workings, the connections, were impossible to reassemble.

The tall one kept at me.

"Your fibers, fingerprints. DNA—they were all over that apartment. On his corpse "

"My DNA?"

The anger flashed in my voice.

My prints, if they'd dusted, sure, they'd find partials on some doorknob. But I'd never touched his body.

"You know damn well I didn't kill anyone." I spoke too loudly. It was what they wanted, for me to spout, careless, incriminate myself. "The place had been cleaned out when I got there. Whoever killed him . . . My guess—"

I stopped. On the tip of my tongue: whoever strung Max up, whoever had scrubbed the place . . .

"Your guess?"

He picked up the receiver. Unspooled the phone cord, pulling it taut. Moore edged closer. A bluff, I thought. They wouldn't kill me, at least not here, now. Then again, maybe Max and Anna had thought the same thing. *They're not going to kill me, not when there's something I might know, useful information.* But maybe their killers had not wanted the knowledge itself, but for that knowledge to go away. Erased not just from the notebooks and hard drives, but the soft tissues of human memory.

"You're guess?" he repeated.

I sputtered, backing off.

"Hite? What the fuck did you want with Hite?"

"I was on assignment, the magazine." They knew this, I suspected. "I thought she might be able to give me something. Some color. But I never found her."

"What kind of color?"

"I never found her," I said again.

He didn't like my answer. Took a step toward me, calm, dead-eyed. He gripped the receiver, dumbbell fashion—as if ready to bludgeon me upside the head. I felt Moore behind me, blocking my way to the door.

Then he pulled his knee up—and pivoted, like a ballplayer, a pitcher on a mound, one arm flailing behind—and hurled the phone against the opposite wall.

The room fell quiet.

He glanced at Agent Moore. Something passed between the two, a shared joke, mutual disdain, a touch of theater.

"That's enough," said Moore.

Gangly Man grew ganglier. He jerked once—like a marionette, not quite under control. He chafed, disliking the other's tone, and I saw it again. These two, their alliance—whatever the underlying exigencies—was built less on unraveling Max's demise (if one or the other had not been involved, or both, through surrogates or otherwise) than on recovering something, or someone, that had slipped out of their reach.

The gangly one succumbed.

"All right," he said. "I'll be outside if you need me."

The afternoon light fell through the door as he left. The sun had scarcely moved. I was surprised how little time had passed. The hour felt later inside the motel, shades drawn, as if the room existed in perpetual dusk. Moore slapped a dossier on the table, an old-fashioned paper file. Mug shots of Hite, slack-jawed, very young, early adolescence, fair-haired; also, vice photos, sitting on the lap of some burly fool—Kiwanis Club, Kearney, Nebraska; then more later, higher class clientele, better dressed, fancier surroundings, though the faces of the men in these latter shots had been blacked out, smudged.

"Why?"

"It's not your issue."

"You're protecting them."

"They're minor figures," he shrugged. "They may think they're important, but they're shills too, puppets."

Something passed over his face, smug, quickly hidden, as if those hidden figures were at his disposal. Suits, too clever by half. Who thought Justice was under their thumb, but really it was the other way around. One of those places I recognized, the Sundial House. Those faces, too, blacked out.

Remove the veil and I might recognize one or two.

Gaddis, maybe.

Myself.

"Regarding Valerie Hite," he said. "After Albuquerque, our documentation on her falls off a cliff. We know she was still in New Mexico, on the fringe of things, when Rolland passed. Then, Omaha. The question, though. Where is she now?"

"I don't know."

"I think you do."

"No."

"You need to find her."

I contemplated surrendering the address Akeesha Ainsley

had given me. but I didn't know if Hite was there now, never mind Moore's intentions.

"Why me?"

"Because you're not one of us. This case—let's just say, we're under pressure. We don't work in a vacuum, not a perfect one. That kind of pressure, the information sharing is not always airtight. You know how it goes."

I knew something about it, competing agencies, agendas at cross-purposes. It had been the same in my father's time—except it wasn't just the Feds and the CIA anymore, but all their stepchildren, a tangled web of enforcement, acronyms to the moon and back. Also, the private firms, their contractors, not to mention the higher ups, the intel committees, the appointees.

The chances for information to leak, to end up someplace other than intended, were all but infinite.

"What you mean," I said. "You can't trust your own people."

A shadow fell across the window: his colleague, pacing. Moore waited for the shadow to pass.

"He never showed me his identification."

Moore gave me a look. The look told me not to push it. Moore was the credentialed one, his cohort deep ops, a foot (maybe both feet), in the criminal underworld, the Bureau's unwholesome allegiances.

Moore didn't say that, of course. It was just a look.

"This is what you need to know," Moore said. "Toward the end of his life, Mikel Rolland had grown disenchanted, and started to document his disenchantment. But then Mikel bumped his head, and that information fell to his son."

Moore pulled up a crime scene photo: Rolland's kid, Zeke, gutted in that far away alley, murdered while soliciting sex from a male prostitute. Moore scoffed at the report. "Don't get me wrong—Rolland's kid was no saint. Congenital criminal, death wish. Whatever you want to say. But it wasn't sex that got Zeke killed. The tabloids got that right."

"What then?"

"Blackmail, attempted. Using information from his father's folio on Sundial." He paused, repeated himself. "Blackmail." he said again. "Trouble was, he tried to extort the wrong people, out of his league. Then Hite got frightened and went underground."

"You think she has the folio?

"That's our intelligence. Let me tell you, straight ahead. From where I sit, my position, Hite can disappear, leave the country, vanish into the ether. No one gives a shit. What I need from you, secure the papers before she vanishes. Do that for us, you can go about your goddamn life."

He wanted a carrier, someone to deliver the information, a person from the outside. Who would hand it over to him, outside the system. So, the handling of the information—who was protected, who exposed, high or low—was at his discretion.

I didn't trust him.

They had me boxed.

Murder charges, scandal. If I betrayed them, played whistle-blower—no would believe a thing I said. I'd end up like Seeghurs.

Meantime, they wanted Hite.

With all their resources, she'd stumbled past them.

I heard footsteps on the concrete stairway outside. A shadow fell across the curtain, the same shadow. Moore went to the door and his gangly partner entered, ducking his head, and the room fell out of proportion around him.

"He's been debriefed?"

"Yes," said Moore.

"What if I refuse?" I asked.

"You won't."

"No," said the other. "He's a family man."
They left me to find my own way home.

PART 6

THE DESERT

TWENTY-THREE

New Mexico, August

—

TWO DAYS LATER, Renée's call caught me in the parking lot outside the Lariat Motel in Albuquerque. The Lariat was Valerie Hite's last known address. I didn't expect to find her here. I was delaying, going through a charade.

The evening moved toward dusk, the light dying, and a young prostitute posed at the corner stop.

"How's Los Angeles?" Renée asked.

I wasn't in Los Angeles. I'd lied. For her safety, the children's. We'd spent a tender evening together before I'd gotten on the plane, I'd been seized by an impending sense of loss, up there on hill, overlooking the Canal, those gray rooftops, back lots strewn with salvage and bougainvillea.

"How's the Ferragamo?" she asked.

The Ferragamo was a hotel in Los Angeles, not far from LAX, a place we both knew from back in the day, where midlevel campaign operatives met their street volunteers—while the bigger shots hit the fundraisers in the hills.

"How's the carpeting?"

"It's still orange, still shag."

"That's impossible."

"Yes, but it's true."

She laughed. We'd fucked on that carpeting, orange shag—just like a lot of other people had, in those giant bean bags, too (candidates and their interns, ambitious aides), but that was a long time ago. I was nowhere near the Ferragamo, and the shag, no doubt, was long gone, too.

She was savvy enough to know this—if she wanted to know. And savvy enough to turn her head.

What she let pass—out of naivete, self-protection, or some other reason less innocent . . . I didn't want to think about.

"Tomorrow, I'm out to the Springs. Some place nicer."

I was going out to meet a client, off-grid, I'd told her. I couldn't say who because that's the way it was sometimes—and she didn't push it. A couple of the campaigns were shaking up staff, not unusual this point in the cycle. It made for opportunities.

"Have you met with anyone yet?"

"You know how it is. They keep you waiting, then keep you some more. But tomorrow, we drive out. Spend time together, one on one."

"How long?"

"A couple days. I'll call you when it's done."

"They serious, you think? Or just stringing you along?"

"A little bit of both."

"People can be two things at once. But not forever."

"No," I said, "of course not."

Though whether either of us believed that, I don't know. We were slow to get off the phone.

THE LARIAT WAS one of those old roadside places along Route 66, left over from the days of the big neon signs. More recently, absentee owners had sold off the giant cowboy and his swirling rope, but it was the same two-story motel, rear windows facing the parking lot and a red arrow pointing to the office around the corner. The young woman still posed at the bus stop, and another sat on a bench outside the office door. The latter pursed her lips as if to speak—a native girl, maybe fourteen, dark skin and pink lipstick—but managed only a sleepy look. She had opioid eyes, and a phoenix tattooed on her arm: the kind of girl Hite had been once.

The woman at the desk studied me to see what kind of rube I was. Or was pretending to be. My guess, the place didn't get too many tourists anymore.

"You looking for a room?"

"A person. A woman."

"We just provide the rooms."

"No, that's not it. I'm looking for someone who worked this area some time back."

"You with vice?"

"No."

"A pimp?"

I showed her pictures from the dossier. She gave them an off-kilter glance. She was a few years older than Hite would be now —with a beaten, no-nonsense look that suggested she'd taken the long way around to her current position. The street trade had drifted off over the last decade, but come back with a vengeance, triggered by the crackdown on online purveyors.

"Did she get away from you?"

"No," I said. "It's not about me and her. I'm looking on behalf of someone else."

"People come to a motel, they got their right to privacy."

I took out some cash.

"That doesn't change my answer."

I made to take the bills away, but she lowered her hand over mine. "What's up with these blurred faces?"

"I guess they don't want to be recognized."

"You working for them?"

"No," I said, though I supposed it could be true. Sometimes in any line of work, you labored for people behind the scenes you didn't know—or pretended not to know.

"For who, then? The family?"

"I can't say."

She shrugged.

"The woman, I've seen a hundred like her. All I can tell you, that last picture—it's Santa Fe."

"Yes."

"The hills—Camel Rock. Out by the Opera House. A runner came down here, like they do sometimes, looking for girls. So, I went. But I didn't fit the bill," she shrugged again, matter of fact. "Lucky me." The shot had been taken at a party, by a pool— a rock formation looming in the hills above. The Sundial House, where Rolland had lived before retreating farther into the desert. Hite stood in the foreground, dressed in summer clothes, hair up —a touch upscale, fashionable, as if dusted with money.

"That's what all the girls want, still. Up to Santa Fe. Everything's off the street there. Always has been. Penetrate that world, you can fuck real money. Basketball players. Movie directors. Steve McQueen."

"Steve McQueen's dead."

"Ben Stiller . . . Mark Zuckerberg . . . Lizard People . . . but your friend—she's past all that."

"What do you mean?"

"Deceased. Or good as. Chained to a wall, a pretty wall,

maybe. Or doesn't want to be found. My advice, unless you're being paid good money—or someone's got you by the balls—let it go."

"I'm afraid I don't have that option."

"That's too bad."

The door chime sounded behind us, and the clerk turned her attention to the couple entering: the native girl with a man about my age, wearing a gold band he hadn't bothered to remove.

I went through the motions, working Hite's old haunts, but my only real lead was the address Akeesha Aimsley had given me, on a rural road, way out in the middle of nothing, snaking into the high country west of Taos. I knew Rolland had retreated out that way toward the end, a small ranch on old hunting grounds, goats and apples, an old kiva on the property, a peyote altar out in the rocks. Maybe this address was the same place, I didn't know for sure, but I didn't want anyone following me. If I found her, I had no idea what would happen: If Moore could keep his crew from intervening, or even intended to. Meantime, the credit card records, the phone stream, the embedded GPS, all still put me right here, right now. Likely they also had someone on the ground, close by.

The next morning, I went off book. I left my phone in the motel and took a taxi out to a private seller I'd found in the library online, an older man, a survivalist, who hustled munitions out of a mobile unit in a retirement community. He sold me a short barrel Springfield and a Faraday pouch: a small bag lined with magnetic foil designed to block the transmission of electronic signals. Back at the motel, I dropped my phone into the Faraday then headed to where the strip broadened, past the apartment buildings, the self-storage, the liquor havens and trailer parks. Out to the land of metal roofs and glare and distant bus shelters. Young women hanging here, too. More stone, more gravel, more dirt. The streets wider and the glare brighter and the motels farther apart until they clustered again out by the cloverleaf.

I pulled into a gas station.

I had options.

The freeway south, to the border. The Mesa out west. Also, the other direction, back through town, toward the distant East.

But if I wanted home . . .

I had to get Moore what he wanted.

That meant north, up 25, toward Santa Fe, then the high road to Taos, snaking upland, and hoping the young woman was still there. It didn't feel likely. And less likely, when I found her, *if* I found her, the Feds wouldn't suddenly converge.

I hesitated at the pump.

I had the phone on the seat beside me, inside the Faraday, a dead signal. I could take the phone out later, or leave it inside the Faraday forever, fade off the map. I touched my pocket, feeling the outline of the short barrel in its pocket holster. The gun in my pocket gave me the same uneasy rush I'd felt years ago. The rush could get you in trouble, but I didn't want to be caught unarmed out in the nowhere.

I sat at the station for long time, until a car pulled into line behind, and a horn blared.

I pulled out.

No one followed, so far as I could tell, but I'd gotten this wrong more than once.

TWENTY-FOUR

—

I HAD BEEN in the New Mexican desert before, years ago, when
my father had been working with the government, on defense
communications systems, at a base outside Las Cruces. Since
then, the place had haunted me. I had felt at the time, and felt
now, that I both did and did not belong there. The system had to
do with the Titan missiles. My father lived with my mother and
sister in a civilian barracks outside town.

I was a young journalist, between jobs, come down to get a
look at the Southwest. My parents had been on their own journey. It was a transitional time for them, not the kind of life my
mother signed on for—six months here, a year there, migrating
from missile site to missile site—but there would be a payoff at
the end, a more prestigious position for my father, travel abroad.
Despite her discontent, she did not take long to blend with the
land, lying in the chaise by the pool in her dark sunglasses. She
wore an ouroboro bracelet, hammered silver, and grew warm in
the sun. The barracks did not look like much: apartments in a
low slung, bright-colored building, freshly built, all angles, a

government-leased motel at the edge of town. Their balcony overlooked the desert, a two-lane running out to the vanishing point: a road down which my father drove in the morning to a base surrounded by concertina wire. The temperature fell sharply at night. My mother would wake up chilled—then go down to warm up in the sun.

"People come to find themselves down here," she said. "That's the rumor."

"Is it true?"

"Ask your father. He's the mystic these days."

I'd noticed my father's restlessness, but he was no mystic. Rather, he was a materialist in the old sense, spirit and matter being irretrievably bound, transformation a thermodynamic process and nothing to trifle with. Still, a few days later he drove me out to the testing grounds at White Sands. We stopped at a roadside bar run by the Mescalero Apache. The Mescalero weren't friendly, but the bar was the only place out here. Located across from Site 22, near the missile range, the bar drew servicemen from Holloman Air Force Base, also engineers from there, truckers, ranch workers, members of the tribe. The disparate groups didn't commingle much. There were suspicions —over what went on at the missile range: alleged cattle mutilations, hovering lights, abducted children.

At the bar we met up with a man my father knew, a defense contractor who had driven out with a young woman from Las Cruces. We climbed into his Jeep and headed toward the range. The contractor insisted the woman drive. He liked looking at her behind the wheel. Also, he needed his hands free, he claimed, so he could smoke and drink.

"You don't need your hands free for that," she said.

"Yes, I do."

The contractor showed his identity card at the gate. He was up in the hierarchy, so the guard waved us through.

"Are you sure we should be out here today?" the woman asked. She was a base hanger, but not the usual kind: the daughter of a congressman, a retired military man who brought defense work to the state. The contractor really shouldn't be messing with her, but he had a reckless streak.

"They let us in, didn't they?"

"It's a missile range," she said. "And there's a launch today."

"Later, this evening. There's no payload."

"From what Dick tells me, sometimes out here, the right hand doesn't know what the left is thinking."

"Is that the kind of thing you tell the congressman's daughter, Dick?" The contractor threw his cigarette out the window. "Not exactly what we want getting back to Washington."

The woman caught my father's eye in the rearview: a big-boned blonde, long lashes and pale lips. She made turquoise jewelry in Las Cruces.

"Also, you lied to the MP. You said we are only going to Site 22."

"I didn't lie," the contractor replied. "He misunderstood. Anyway, I'm in charge."

"No, you're not. You're a civilian."

"Haven't you heard? It's a democracy. Civilians are in charge of everything, including your father, the congressman, people's servant. Two years from now, he'll need a bumper sticker to remember his name."

We had already passed Site 22, a hill with a view back toward the proving ground. She kept driving—at the contractor's insistence—all the way to Trinity, to where the road stopped at the edge of the nuclear crater. An obelisk marked the spot. The sand at the heart of the explosion had liquified, leaving a glass residue, a green sheet, miles wide, splintering, cracked and broken at the edges by souvenir hunters.

"They make this into jewelry," said the woman.

"Take some more. Fill your purse."

"The sign says no. It's illegal."

"Fuck the sign."

Before the blast, the army had gathered enlisted men, some in bunkers, some out in the open, soldiers glad to be on duty anywhere but the Pacific: better here than the unfinished war, island hopping to remove every Japanese soldier from every cave. Some of the GI's had died shortly after the test, irradiated, same as in Hiroshima, and others came down with carcinomas, lesions, that didn't show up till years later.

The woman teared up.

"I don't want to be here anymore."

She handed the keys to my father and climbed into the back. The contractor climbed back with her, and I rode in the passenger seat alongside my father. We drove past the building where Oppenheimer had supervised the blast, then back through the heat and sand all the way to Mescalero.

Indians in cowboy hats drank whiskey and smoked cigarettes out front.

One hissed, a snake noise. The contractor puffed his chest, offended, but the Apache ignored him.

The man ranted anyway.

"They think they have been displaced. Well, we've all been displaced. Same monkey, same story. They think they emerged from the underground, the First People, but they were cliff dwellers, tiny people climbing naked on the rocks. Then the aliens came."

"Stop," the woman said.

He didn't listen.

"Visitors." He pointed to the sky. "From the stars. Refugees, colonizers. Snakes with opposable thumbs. The aliens couldn't survive on the surface of our dear planet. So, they dragged the Apache into the center of the earth and fucked the shit out of 'em. Not all of them, of course. That would have been a lot of work, to fuck every monkey on earth." He was a charming man.

The Indians said nothing. They stared through us as if we didn't exist. We got into my father's car. Drove across the highway to the top of Hill 22. Time did funny things out here in the desert. The man kept talking.

We stepped out.

The woman started to puke.

"But we were transformed. Some of us, anyway. We scratched things on rocks. We mounted horses."

The others were drunk by now. Me, too. The man kept rattling. Something darted into a hole in the sand. The contractor might have gone on all night, but a light streamed out of the south: a sound like the sky tearing, cloth ripping at the seams, one world emerging out of another, more light, a quick searing, a giant puff of white smoke, followed by a slow rolling thunder.

A test rocket.

The Trident, moving by guidance system toward the Sangre de Cristo. A navy missile, but tested out here in the desert, launched from a platform in the salt flats the other end of White Sands. It triggered calls to the police, chatter on the CB, a wave of speculation on late night radio. Also, news stories, unconfirmed, about a rancher who'd driven to the top of a ridge, within sight of an alien craft, only to be turned away by the National Guard.

I looked at my dad.

"I thought you might want to see," he said.

We dropped the contractor at his Jeep, and the woman rode back with us. My father stopped the car on the way and vomited into the desert sand. It was late when we got back to Las Cruces. He drove the woman home without asking for directions.

She leaned into the car window.

"I've lived here all my life . . . it isn't just visitors, locals too, something unseen. People get this idea in their head, like they've been chosen . . ." She tilted her chin to the sky, and the darkness fell on her face, and the starlight, too, both at once. She was closer to my age than his. "I feel like sometimes I've been chosen, too, like someone's watching. Only they never come."

When we got to our apartment, my father didn't kill the engine. He looked worn, a man at odds with himself. His quest, his search, his shadow . . . out there at the crater. That reflection in the green trinitite, cast across the blasted sand.

"I have to go out to the base."

My mother and sister sat on the couch in front of the television. They'd been shopping while we were out and gotten some antlers and a kachina doll. Robert Redford climbed up a sheer cliff, pressed flat to a rock wall, knife between his teeth, headed toward a sniper in a cave.

I felt like I'd seen the movie before, but maybe I hadn't. Either way, it wasn't hard to guess what was going to happen. "There's something deeper going on," my mother said. She ran her fingers over the kachina doll, admiring it in a heartbroken way. Outside the desert night was dark. I went to the window.

There was no wind.

There were no shadows.

The road was long and empty.

TWENTY-FIVE

▭

GoaTs for SALe

THE ADDRESS **A**KEESHA had given me led to a sign hanging on a locked cattle guard across from a mileage marker in the rural highlands. I ducked under and followed the dirt road to a clearing, a shuttered house, wood frame, weathered, the color all but leached from the surface. It looked to have been shuttered for a while. The house stood downslope of an aging apple orchard. I couldn't see the goats, but I could hear them braying.

I circled the empty house, a modest dwelling, a simple place out on the ridge looking toward the reservation. There was evidence of Mikel Rolland's hand: a stone sundial, cantilevered into the garden, and an outdoor bath, basalt, fed by a water tank, bone dry now. The bath was not large but still a luxury, given the water situation, more so lately, with the successive years of drought, and the unpredictability of the desert monsoons. The summer thunderheads built up in the afternoons, letting loose suddenly, threatening to wash everything away, but there was no sign of that now. The sky was cloudless and empty. Just light fading and fading some more. A small animal skittered off into the scrub under a domestic succulent gone wild, a violent spike of color in the blue grass. Rolland apparently hadn't stopped entertaining, not entirely. There were the remains of a patio, rusted lanterns and furniture gone desiccate, and it wasn't hard to imagine the parties here, celebrities stuttering about in the moss rock and malpais.

After his wife died, all that had stopped. His son came and went. Also, a spiritual advisor, name of Manuel Nunez: the kiva tender.

A ceremonial kiva, peyote.

I walked toward the goats, toward their clattering and braying down in the hollow. A young man emerged from the barn, and another man, older, regarded me from behind a pickup truck: a big-shouldered man, long black hair pulled into a ponytail.

"You looking for some goats?"

I wished it were that simple, but I figured, just looking at me, he knew it wasn't true. I told him I was looking for a woman named Valeria Hite. Who had spent some time out here. And maybe recently returned.

"What makes you think that?"

"A friend of hers, she gave me the address. Also, a colleague of mine," I paused, wondering how deep to go. "He entrusted me with a few items, valuables—to pass along."

I carried the envelope I'd taken from Coney Island, and the Springfield, too, holstered in my pants pocket, up front, a deep pocket: a small gun with a light action safety on the trigger. Noticeable, but compact enough, in its pocket holster. It might have been a phone, a pack of cigarettes, a box of Altoids, any damn thing.

"You came alone?"

"Yes."

I didn't know if he believed me. Or if I were certain myself. He spoke to the younger man in Spanish, sending him up the hill on his motorcycle to look around.

"You might have known her under another name. She was friends with Rolland's son."

"That was my father's arrangement," he said. "He and Mikel got along. We have only so much by way of water rights here—and Mikel, he made a deal with the Pueblo—for more water. But now, my father's dead, Mikel, too, and that's dried up. It's a trickle. The goats, the horses, the apples, they all need water. We have enough for the animals or the apples, but not both."

He was maybe fifty years old, skin leathered from the sun. His hair was jet black. He might have been part Indian, but his resemblance wasn't to the Pueblo, and his accent suggested somewhere else. There was a Mennonite dove engraved over the barn door. The group had a community over the border, Spanish speaking, so maybe it was that. He wore a tool belt about his waist—fencing pliers, a hammer—but also, in that holster, a gun.

"For snakes," he said.

Another house stood farther on, the main house, modest—and beyond that, various outbuildings, sheds, a cluster of migrant housing: a patchwork of wood and stucco and corrugated tin. It was hard, from this distance, to tell if it were occupied.

"She was," I repeated, "friends with his son."

"Zeke. The kid was a handful."

"She was part of his entourage, there at the end."

"Entourage," he scoffed. "People tell their stories, but there was never any entourage out here. Just us. My dying father, up there in the apple picker cabins."

"Nunez, too?"

I asked because I'd come across Nunez in the Feds' report—as someone in Rolland's circle back then. The aging actress had mentioned him, too, that evening when we stood by the black-bottom pool out at Sundial. Nunez was a peyote roadman, a Pueblo Indian who had later lost his status in the tribe for conducting the peyote ceremony off reservation. He'd worked under different names—Ignacio Cloud Dragon, aka Richard Mendez, aka Ralph Milan—and the DEA had gotten involved. "We don't see him much anymore. The Pueblo won't have anything to do with him. So, he's with the Apache now, in and out, doing what he's always done, only more under the radar. Up to Dulce."

The sky was empty and the air hot. There was no wind, not much movement, just the goats grazing, chewing, and a donkey stomping around behind a battered fence. The motorcycle grew loud again, and the young rider reappeared on the gravel road, cutting the engine when he got close.

"Anything?" the rancher asked.

"Just this guy's car."

"Anyone else?"

"Not so far as I could tell."

The rancher wasn't reassured. He touched his gun, then hissed at the barn again—summoning a different boy, younger (another son, I figured)—in Spanish again: a dialect I couldn't quite grasp, tinged with German, Dutch, whatever the Mennonites clung too. The kid hurried past us toward the house.

"Come with me."

The rancher and I walked up the hill past a stone ranch house—tin roof, an older woman on the porch, rocking—toward the small cluster of migrant housing, chickens out front. The kid scurried farther on. The rancher stayed to my right, the gun side, a half step behind. Eyes downcast, watching my hands. I kept them away from my pocket.

"This way," he said.

We went down a path, away from the housing, into the scrub

alongside a rock shelf. He dropped a little farther behind me. A cliff rose to one side, hollowed, a natural chimney at one end; also, a depression in the floor, fissured and broken, a gap wide enough to glimpse the escarpment below. A natural shelter, along an old hunting trail: a rock formation that evoked the old ceremonial kivas.

"Peyote," said the rancher. "Nunez kept those ceremonies small, low-key, but some people have a hard time of it. Depending on their nature, their state of mind. Before his death, Mikel, one of those ceremonies, he got lost in the malpais."

Then I heard something behind us and caught the cast of his eyes down the path. I followed that cast and saw the woman. I didn't recognize her at first. The kid must have retrieved her from those cabins and sent her down. She dressed simply, jeans, a dust-colored shirt, hair pulled back, slim-hipped, boyish, nothing exclamatory about her—aside from her sudden appearance—just a woman, slump shouldered, indistinguishable. Except for the mottled complexion, the black eyes.

Neither of us spoke. A hawk circled overhead, a large bird, iron gray.

I pulled the envelope from my back pocket and handed it to her. It held the documents: the passport under the name of Maggie Highsmith; and that letter from the Banco Internacional —instructions on how to access the cash account at a teller's window, any Banco Internacional, a Mexican bank with offices all over the world: popular with travelers who wanted to drop below the radar, cash only, no credit receipts to trace. I knew Seeghurs had made such arrangements in the past, digging into his resources to arrange cover for a source.

"The folio," I said. "You promised Max—"

"Why didn't he come himself?"

I told her.

She studied the dirt, looked up.

The way she regarded me, I saw her previous identities at once: the wholesome counselor, Dorothy Waters, and her earlier self, the street girl, Valerie Hite. She possessed a rangy, raw-boned charm, inherent in the duality, in the way she held herself —at once haughty, prim, rough around the edges. On the verge of this new identity, the woman in the passport. I told her the bargain I'd made—in that the motel in the Canal District. And what might happen to me if I didn't come through.

"You can disappear however you want. I don't need to know," I said. "But I need the folio."

The rancher shuffled his feet behind me. I understood why he'd taken me out here, away from the cabins, The countryside was vast, the path fell into the arroyo. If things got dicey, a gunshot might echo a long way, but nobody would think anything of it.

He ordered me to the ground, face first, then searched me, spread-eagled in the dirt.

Later, I drove through the apple orchard in the dark, up the gravel grade to the state highway. Valerie Hite rode in the passenger seat, and the rancher followed in a squared-off sedan whose lights lurched with every bump in the road. Hite had been Dorothy Waters back in Omaha, but we weren't in Omaha, and out here, in the desert, that woman no longer existed and her new self was yet to be. So she was Hite. And she had my gun inside her purse, and her hand in there, too. Also, my cell, still in its Faraday. The sedan lurched behind us until we hit the two-lane, then stayed close on the asphalt, swinging up behind as we hit the junction near Taos.

"To the left," Hite said. "North."

"Where are we going?"

"Dulce. But we must stop along the way."

There was an Apache casino in Dulce, also an airstrip. According to the rancher, Nunez piloted in and out several times a year—and sometimes met with old clients, though not as openly as before.

"I can drive wherever you need," I said. "I can stall getting back. Delay. Give you as much time as you need to get off the grid. All I need is those papers . . . the folio."

"Why should I trust you?"

"I have a wife, a daughter."

"That's a new one," she said. "I never heard that one before."

I heard a West Nebraska wind in her voice, the empty buttes, the lost heartland. I knew there was more to her personal history—but I didn't ask for the details. I'd already explained the reason I'd sought her out—and what the agents wanted. I started through it again. She shook her head. "I was doing okay in Omaha," she said. "I had a life. No one would have come looking for Dorothy Waters, or knew she existed, if Seeghurs hadn't led them to me."

We were north of Taos, headed toward the gorge ahead.

I kept driving.

She kept her hand in the purse, on the gun, and touched the cross on the chain around her neck, same gesture as Akeesha Aimsley. It didn't reassure me. Working crime, the meth fields, I'd seen gangbangers cross themselves before driving off to murder the kid three blocks over.

The Rio Grande was just ahead.

"Pull over."

We'd lost the rancher some time back. A car went by, but it wasn't him. She commanded me farther off the road, sideways into the gravel.

The rancher pulled up. The light wheeled on her face, shadows—the innocent girl who'd grown up in trailer parks, the prostitute, extortionist, youth counselor, churchgoer—you could project anything you wanted onto her, like plenty of people had done, men, women, as she surrendered herself beneath them, or feigned surrender. While the rest of us, you, me, features smudged, lingered out by the pool.

She took the gun from her purse.

"Hand me the keys," she said.

The rancher pulled my suitcase from the car.

The three of us stood darkly on the concrete walkway, next to the guardrail, on the high bridge spanning the Rio Grande. The plateau stretched far and dark, no trees, just desert scrub, darker on the horizon, except for headlights, way out there, moving along a curvature that made it hard to judge the cars' distance. The river knifed through the gorge below us.

Hite removed my phone from the Faraday bag.

"I don't know if that's such a good idea."

"We're taking you off the grid."

She handed me the phone.

"Call your wife," the rancher said.

I didn't get it.

"I was already off the grid," I said. "You just put me back on."

The headlights on the horizon became more distinct, a car approaching, closing quickly, then the curvature carried the same lights farther away. The road was not as straight as it seemed. "Just call your wife," he repeated. "Leave a message. Car trouble. Out in the middle of nowhere. Waiting for assistance. You just want her to know."

"They'll track my call."

"Just do as I tell you," said the rancher.

Hite held the Springfield. There was a safety on the trigger, like a Glock, but the trigger itself was light action, an easy pull. Too easy, maybe. Anxious shooters, unholstering, sometimes pulled past the safety and fired unintentionally. A cop or three had shot themselves in the thigh. So the seller had told me, fair warning, but not until he'd taken my money. The bit about the cops had amused him.

"What if she picks up?" I asked.

"No one picks up anymore."

"She's my wife."

"It's late," Hite added, as if that ended it; wife or no, all calls went to voice after a certain hour. "But she picks up, you can handle it . . . you know how to talk."

She explained again what they wanted me to say: how I was out here, broken down, waiting for help. Then the headlamps of that distant car emerged from the long curve, the distance collapsing. The driver slowed at the bridge. Our shadows grew in the light. Now was the time, if I meant to take a chance, to dart out, wave it down—but I didn't. Too much could go wrong.

The car gunned by.

I listened to Renée's voice on the message, cheerful and professional, the remnants of Missouri, those flattened vowels roaming the embassy hallways, calm, practical, then lilting of a sudden. I thought about the Frenchman and his Peugeot.

Renée

The line clicked. A noise in the transmission, a flutter in the stars, Renée picking up—but no . . . It was late, she was asleep, or out with Rouche, Lille, those people from the embassy—and had let the message go to voice. I stumbled through it, what they wanted me to say. Another car appeared on the horizon, another set of headlights riding the road around the rim of the earth.

Renée.

The rancher took the cell from my hand. "Now take off your jacket and hand it to Valerie."

Hite dropped the jacket into the chasm. Then my suitcase, with most of my clothes—my pack, my computer. Finally, the phone. She hurled it over the bridge into the gorge. I felt my old existence fading, Renée, the kids. The oncoming headlamps, the new set, still distant, grew brighter, then receded around that long bend. The river wasn't wide here, but it ran swiftly, rapids etching the chasm ever deeper, narrower, into the desert rock. If anyone followed the signal, it would lead them here, to the bottom of the ravine.

We walked on the gravel shoulder by the side of road. The new car reemerged suddenly from the long black curve, a sling-shot of light and noise thundering over the bridge. Then it was gone. The rancher drove away in my rental and left us with the sedan.

"Where's he going?"

"Down the road. Chop shop. Friends in the business. Happens all the time out here. Someone breaks down by the side of road. A good Samaritan happens along, turns out not to be so good after all. Jacks the car, robs the driver . . . Sometimes, the victim shows up after a long walk. Other times, no. Clothes, maybe, teeth. In some ravine, desert canyon. Cops look for a little while, but then they give up."

I saw the dodge. I'd been carjacked, disappeared.

"The Feds—"

"He's not going to turn us in, that's what you're thinking. I sat with his father while he was dying. I was a junkie, but I still sat with the old man. We have a bond."

"The Feds," I repeated. "Will they buy it—?"

"Some people, trouble in their lives, they arrange the disap-pearing themselves. The cops know that. Feds too. Worst case, they smell bullshit, but they still have to look. Dig around the ravine. Bring out the copters. It buys time."

TWENTY-SIX

THE ONLY HOTEL in Dulce was the Blue Stallion, a casino hotel owned by the Jicarilla Apache. The casino lay in the shadow of Archuleta Mesa, a sheer plateau rising abruptly out of the high desert. Dulce was a small town, a few hundred dwellings scattered over what had once been Agua Dulce, a high desert valley fed by a spring on the other side of a wagon road, now Route 64. A handful of frame houses remained along Basket Lane, but most people lived in trailers and prebuilts. Past the small valley, the reservation land was rocky, inarable for miles. Minerals and timber kept the tribe going—and the casino.

Welcome Southwest Rodeo! & Alien Nation

The rodeo riders had come from the Southwest reservations —bronc riders, barrel racers, steer wrestlers, ropers—so the lobby was crowded, tribal people mostly, families and powwow dancers, though a handful of others, mostly white, were here for a concurrent event, smaller, that catered to the alien trade, so-called, people who came to get a look at Archuleta Mesa, alleged site of Dulce Base, an underground facility hollowed into the plateau, six layers deep, a secret project of the U.S. government and an alien intelligence, which by various means—in various forms, corporal or otherwise—harvested the energy of the human race for purposes not altogether benign. The notion was based on sightings, decades old. Out here in the high desert—the light and shadow—the heat shimmer over the yellow sand, white mesas under the moon, the vast distances—all that made for a sky out of which anything might appear, and the reports continued. Watchers still gathered on the old Gomez Ranch, and Manuel Nunez came in a few times a year to perform his spirit ceremony. He was not Apache but gave a vigorish to the tribe under the auspices of the hotel.

Valerie Hite had the ability to blend in, a chameleon nature, the result of her profession, years in hiding. In the parking lot, she put on a necklace, nice but not too nice, also some shades. She dropped her hair, then tethered it back. A look, together with the simple blouse, the jeans, which would blend with the other passers-through. She counted on the small things, the misdirection.

We waited in line at the desk.

The tribal police glanced us over, a cursory glance. A white couple sat nearby, both wearing name tags: a woman in a gray skirt, a notepad in her lap, and a man beside her, sloppier, in a T-shirt and khakis.

The line dwindled slowly.

"We are here for the Spirit Ceremony," Hite told the clerk "As guests of the tribe. With Manuel Nunez."

Nunez was her way out, through the tribal airstrip, but that window was closing. He'd be gone soon.

Meanwhile, there was paperwork, a transaction. It took time. The pair of us together, at the front desk, I feared, drew attention. I left her to deal with the formalities and went into the casino, a modest space, slots only, then through some double doors into the lounge. I ended up next to a couple at the bar, an older blonde, bright-eyed, and her white-haired husband.

"Were you at the presentation?"

"I'm not sure what you mean."

"You're not here for the rodeo? And you don't play the slots?"

"No."

"Well, you didn't miss much. It was a bit tedious. Dry as dust, really. The new crop, they take this all very seriously. Conspiracy theorists, claiming hard evidence. Or cultural anthropologists, come to study the fruitcakes."

I remembered the other couple in the lobby, their name tags, the woman in her gray skirt, her notepad, the studious manner. She and her rumpled husband.

"Which category are you?"

The woman smiled, good natured. "Actually, all that—it's the sideshow. We come down here to see Manuel Nunez."

She was in her sixties, maybe older. I could see the face work, too much, depending on how you felt about such things— but she carried it off. She had her beauty. Her husband seemed considerably older, a mild-mannered man who wore a hearing aid but made little pretense of following the conversation. "We've been coming out for years," she said. "Ever since our daughter passed." Her eyes stayed cheerful. They'd met Nunez in Los Angeles, she explained, at the house of a friend who'd flown him out to do a healing ceremony. He had been a great help to them, but now, the way things were—Manuel traveling in tighter circles, under scrutiny—contact was more limited.

The drink went to my head. I should seek out Valerie—we were bound together, like it or not—but the old man had already waved his hand in a circle, motioning for another round. The woman talked about how Nunez had to be more careful now. The Apache had two reservations in New Mexico, another in Arizona, each with its own airstrip, but the Feds circled around. Also, DEA, ICE, whoever else. There were meth labs in the tribal canyons, dropped in by helicopter, and illegals in the uranium mines. Nunez had nothing to do with that, she said, but the cops, they had careers to make, quotas to fill.

"Did you lose someone . . .?"

I faltered, unsure what she was after. Her eyes misted. Thinking about her daughter.

"I'm sorry," she said. "I make assumptions. It's just usually, that's how it starts. There's some loss . . . someone close . . . some unnamable part of yourself."

I stood with the smokers outside the casino and considered the desert two-lane running west through Farmington. I'd already circled the lot, examining the rancher's sedan in daylight, an old model, not in great shape. Who knew how far it would get? I lit another cigarette, blending with the gamblers, bleary folks taking a break between slots: tourists and natives, hunters and passers-through, bruised rodeo riders, powwow queens, alien conventioneers. Then Hite came through the lobby door.

"I got the room."

"Your suitcase?

She wore the purse, satchel style, slung over her shoulder. Others regarded her, her mottled beauty, innocence mixed with something harder; it was difficult to tell what was veneer and what lay underneath.

"I already took it in. While you were in the bar."

We walked down the hall. Inside the room, the closet was open, and her suitcase stood on the floor. The room held twin beds and a view of the Archuleta, the high red bluff, the sky blue and full of light. This side of the window, through the gauze curtain and tinted glass, the room existed in the same perennial twilight as the motel down in the Canal. I nodded toward the mesa.

"Is that where Nunez conducts the ceremony?"

"There's a hogan, out by the airstrip."

"The folio?"

"We're on the hotel shuttle, tomorrow, out to the ceremony. By the strip. It's the only way." There were small engine flights, she told me, that ran between this reservation and the Chiricahua strip at the border. Nunez had come in on one of these and would leave the same way.

"The car?"

"What about it?"

"The keys? I'm going to need my own way out of here."

"Tomorrow."

"And the folio?"

"In the closet," she said. "The motel safe."

I saw she had no intention of giving it over until her passage was clear. She still had my gun.

"Is there anything in there worth the fuss?"

"Zeke, after his father died, he rummaged his dad's files. I'm not sure, really, that he knew what he was looking for. But he took part of it. For proof.

"Proof of what."

"His father's money, a big part, was tied up in the foundation. And he didn't want to get locked out. He wanted leverage, but the details, he didn't give them—and I didn't ask. Zeke was reckless."

"You and Zeke . . ."

She shook her head.

"There was nothing between us that way. Zeke liked to make

a show of himself on the strip. He and I, we had some of the same habits." She paused, letting me guess what that might mean. "He had pocket money, plenty, so it was different for him. The drugs, the scams . . . but the game he was playing at the end, I wanted nothing to do with that."

She fell silent again. The sun was a long time across the sky.

"Zeke and I bilked plenty of folks, I admit. Little folk, mostly, the in-betweens. I enjoyed it, so did he. Zeke was a charmer."

"He didn't need the money."

"No, but I did," she said. "He could be a prick. But he got me off the street, out there to the goat ranch. They were good to me out there. I liked the goats, the horses."

"There aren't any horses."

"There used to be. And Nunez, he helped me get straight." She glanced at the closet. "I didn't say I was a good person."

TWENTY-SEVEN

▭

WE WENT OUT the next afternoon, on the hotel shuttle, to a rodeo corral on the other side of the Jicarilla Highway. The crowd came from reservations all over the old Borderlands and stayed the duration, not in the casino hotel, but in tents and campers on the fairgrounds, or on the creek along the highway. Trucks circled the powwow ring. Families ornamented themselves for the dance. Tribal vendors sold jewelry and T-shirts and snakeroot and dreamcatchers and snow cones and Navajo chili from tables and teepees and the trunks of their cars. Ours was a reticent group, disinclined toward purchasing—or tourist gawkery—but the couple from Los Angeles made no pretense. The woman wore a jacket full of shimmer, her aging husband, a high Stetson with an eagle feather. They didn't care who saw them, they bought, they squandered, in a kind of magical light. The contingent from the Midwest hung back, concealing their pale skin and flabbiness and gullibility, but with a slouch that said their gullibility wasn't something to be fucked with. The nervous woman from the lobby had shed the gray skirt and her name tag, but carried the same skeptical expression, aloof, as if watching from behind a screen. She taught at Marquette, she'd announced on the shuttle. Her husband hung close by her, continuing some old argument. They seemed at once horribly separate and inviolably bound.

"It's *not* just a metaphor," he said.

"Maybe not for the Natives, the believers," she said. "But for rest of us, it's a hobby, it's a goddamn T-shirt."

"You're too cynical."

The woman from Los Angeles dropped back, her blonde hair bound in a new scarf—a Navajo pattern—and showed me a necklace, colorful beads, strung in alternating colors meant to evoke the desert pájaro. The firebird had appeared to her in a vision once upon a time.

"My spirit guide," she said. "What they show us is not always what we want to see. Our true nature . . ." she hesitated. "Rumor is they are running sweeps."

"Who?"

"Border agents, narcotics," she shrugged. "But there are always rumors like that."

Hite hung back.

It was better, we decided, to keep a distance. The Feds, if they'd gotten wise, would be looking for a couple.

The shuttle would be reboarding soon.

She still hadn't given me anything. I had no guarantee. I could call her bluff, but it was too late for that.

I'd already cast my lot.

TWENTY-EIGHT

▭

WE SKIRTED THE MESA. We skirted, too, the long fire road to the top of the hill and the radio tower. A gleaming piece of aluminum refuse caught the desert light and led visitors below to speculate as to the source of that light. A door up there into the inner world of the mesa?

"It's *not* just debris," said the professor's husband.

"It's a piece of sheet metal. Discarded when they built the tower."

"That's an opinion."

"I have a picture."

"It's immaterial. It doesn't matter. Pictures can be faked."

It was an argument of the type I'd heard before. In belief, there are people who take everything literally, and those who regard things in a more figurative light. For them, it doesn't matter into which mountainside the door has been carved, or even if the door has a physical reality, only that it exists, in a way that perhaps has little to do with dimensions as we usually perceive them.

Then there is the darker suspicion, suppressed, unexpressed, that there is no door at all, real or imagined.

The shuttle lurched, rolled on.

We drove the paved road until the pavement ran out. The gravel became rutted, the road steeper and more circuitous, then pummeled down to a ravine edged by a barbed fence. The fence marked the boundaries of the reservation. The road narrowed until it became too narrow to drive, and we got out to walk. The tribal patrol pulled into the dust behind us, and two Apache checked our identification. It was pretty much cursory, as we had already been cleared by the hotel—but this part of the reservation was generally off-limits to outsiders. I edged back to help the aging blonde and her white-haired husband. The two Indian cops talked as if we weren't there:

The Feds are making noise.

They're always making noise. Honk, honk. Run, run. But we are an independent nation.

Not so far as the DEA is concerned. Or Immigration. They don't much like your friend down there, Nunez. Respectable Jicarilla don't eat peyote anymore.

It's peaceful business. Cultural tourism. People might not like it, but it pays the bills.

You only say that because you are a peyote eater yourself.

Paid security, side work. You know that. I ride patrol for them, on Wuju the horse. Gathering up wanderers at dawn.

Wrong step, you'll pay a price.

I know what I'm doing.

That's what they all say.

———

THE YOUNGER INDIAN drove off in his patrol car, and the older one led us down the trail. Hite kept some distance between us.

The taste of peyote . . . snake leaping out of the chest . . .

Puke . . .

Buckets of light.

Black sky.

Time grew sloppy out in the desert.

Now . . .

Then . . .

I thought about Mikel Rolland, lost in the malpais, and understood the desire to peer inside of oneself.

Hite passed around the corner ahead, out of view.

Shadows lined the canyons.

We were not in the hogan, not yet. Eyes on me, an interloper. Suspect, in their eyes. I feared. More suspect, if I let the bowl pass.

But that moment had not come.

We had just hit the trail. The shuttle passengers fell silent past the gate, and there was for an instant an immense quietude in which it seemed our physical selves were mere shells, illusions, and we didn't quite exist.

Just the path.

The journey.

The watcher within.

Our own demons.

▭

The trail dropped into a canyon, boxed on one side by the mesa, a landscape full of recesses, opening without warning into a dying bosque: a thin canopy of green over a dry wash, the remains of a small ranch, gray timbers collapsing onto themselves, but also a Quonset hut, open on both sides. A Jeep road serviced the area, snaking back toward the airstrip, a faint line of asphalt visible from the last crest. It was a rustic setup, a remote copse fed by an underground trickle—a seasonal well whose season had ended. Nunez's crew had trucked in water and put up a handful of canvas tents, brightly painted. The Quonset served as the hogan. Not a traditional setup, but Nunez wasn't bound by such things. There were maybe forty of us altogether, along with Nunez and his pilot and a handful of helpers, Navajo, Apache, Pima. Nunez didn't have the look of a mendicant, or of a seer. He wasn't charismatic, at least on the surface, and there was no special light in his eye: a smallish, wide-faced man, in a white-ribbed shirt and jeans. People approached him with little sense of ceremony, the Angelenos, tribal elders, a pregnant woman, a Navajo rider in rodeo chaps. Most of them he seemed to know, but some he didn't: the professor from Marquette (anthropology, it turned out), suddenly shy with humility, her swelling husband, and a pale-faced kid ugly as a loon, a purple-haired soldier, a bald woman in camo, a young man too young for his prison tattoo and his mouthful of yellowing teeth.

Hite went up to him.

Nunez greeted her. A warm greeting, though not without some reserve. No matter their past, this now, the act of ferrying her out, was a transactional matter and carried an element of risk. They stepped through the open end of the Quonset.

Wandered down the dirt road.

Toward a man in an aviator jacket, leaning against a Jeep.

Nunez's pilot, as it turned out.

Whatever arrangement was made next was out of my sight, the other side of that Jeep.

Hite returned first.

Then Nunez.

The man in aviator jacket stayed with the Jeep.

The ceremony unfurled slowly, with little sense of urgency. A woman tended a fire in a moon-shaped altar at the mouth of the Quonset. A young man put out food in ceremonial dishes, small bits of sweet meat and honey masa meant to cut the bitter taste of the peyote. Locals and familiars, the Angelenos among them, added finishing touches to the spirit circle, a geometric pattern created from colored rocks and grain. People sat on cushions around the circle, kneeled, lounged, gathering several rows deep, and beyond the circle, others leaned, chatted, squatted against the Quonset walls. Peyote appeared, a bitter mash in a large bowl, cactus stripped of its rind. A drummer started up, very faintly, and after a bit the fire woman—still tending the fire, her back to us—sang a song, chanting, a wavering cry, issued from the back of her throat, unimpeded by sense.

The peyote made the rounds. I was on the path again, watching from the elsewhere. A large book rested on a card table covered with white cloth. Nunez had been a peyote roadman for a long time, both within the tradition and without. Though the book lay open, he didn't glance at the page. He chanted to the Great Spirit in a mix of languages—Navajo, Spanish, English, Athabaskan—all mingling off his tongue. Remnants of missionary Catholicism, native belief.

Evoking Genesis.

Evoking the child in the womb, suspended in darkness but able to hear those voices on the other side of the membrane, beckoning:

Let there be light.

Nunez's voice was not electric, nor forceful. He spoke softly while an assistant rolled tobacco and passed the cigarettes into the circle. Then more forcefully.

Ge' shoo!

He went on speaking.

How the spirit manifests itself in many ways. How the eagle may appear to be separate from the rabbit from the vermin in the grass, but it is an illusion, each continually changing form, consumed one by the other, while seeking to endure. The spirit exists in rebellion with itself, age-old. Stars hurling themselves from the sky, Ezekiel's chariot spitting fire, light falling into crevices and cracks, serpents slithering into the earth. Reemerging in other forms.

His face grew fearsome.

He shook the rattle. He'd been called a con, a white man posing as a Mestizo posing as a Pueblo who had been outcast and made an Apache—not by the true elders but the criminal element. Nonetheless, the Quonset air shimmered. The rattle was in the shape of a snake, beads in the tail, poised as if to strike, venom in the fangs, peyote in the venom. He passed the rattle into the crowd. Then came something akin to testifying. People took the rattle and they spoke. They sang the praise, but also the lament. But mostly, they spoke their desires. They wanted contact with ancestors, with the dead. With their estranged mother, their brother lost in Iraq, a grandchild taken by social services. They wanted freedom from material. They wanted to be rid of the ghosts who inhabited their house. To be free from the aliens who had crawled up out of the caves beneath Dulce and dragged their children into bondage. They wanted proof of that which was eluding them. They wanted more from peyote than shimmering image and puke.

Hite stood alone at the back of the Quonset—by the cushions, sleeping rolls, neat bundles.

The wand came to me. I shook the rattle. I listened to the chanting, to the keening. The keening rose within me, unintelligible. I passed the stick and saw the shapes in the pebbles and the rocks, forming, not forming, and then the nausea came. I weaved my way outside and crawled into the brush. I was sick. Everything came up. I watched the smoke curl away from the fire woman's altar and the shapes shift in the flames and listened to the chanting.

I wandered into the desert, into the expanse under the night sky. The jagged outcroppings of the Archuleta shadowed the darkness—creased by the moon, by sudden splashes of white rock. A calm came over me. The arms of the cacti, long spines, rocks, my shoes, fingers, all etched in a sudden clarity. I was no longer outside the Archuleta, but inside. I had gone through the door, and was *deep* inside, beneath the alien base, just me, on my knees, staring into the shimmering pond on the desert floor.

The surface was black. I searched that surface looking for my reflection . . . sifting through the sand . . . a shadow in the depths slipping through my fingers.

Something scuttled in the brush.

I wandered in the dark. The canvas tents were just the other side of the Jeep road, people gathered farther down, by the vehicles, shadows wandering. A light appeared on the road, a motorcycle, and the motorcyclist dismounted and joined some others by the supply trailer. I sat near the tent, invisible on a rock, indistinguishable from the shadows. I heard voices.

They're coming. A dawn raid.

Who?

Who do you think?

Feds?

After Nunez—he's wanted for trafficking.

Bullshit.

I lay in the same spot as when I'd left the hogan, retching in the grass. Hite leaned over me. A couple of men stayed behind, shadows: Nunez, his white shirt, I recognized, and the other one, the pilot. There were more, suddenly close, then gone, footsteps hissing along. I felt my vulnerability—an outsider, on a mission for the Feds, someone it may be wise to eliminate—but these passing shadows didn't know me from the dirt, and Nunez was no killer. Hite leaned closer. *Inside the Quonset, next to the sleeping cots. What you came for. Under a jacket by the wall. But*

don't fool around here. Go. Take the path out the way we came.
The fire woman still nursed the fire, but the fire was smaller. A
car door slammed. I saw taillights along the Jeep road, the lights
growing larger as the Jeep reached the crest, as if taking flight, a
red gleam streaking across the sky, then flaming out.

A peyote blur.

Followed, later, as I got to my feet, by a sound like night
thunder echoing in the desert canyons.

The plane?

People wondered. There was a small commotion, a handful,
curious, headed up the dark rise, but not much to see.

Inside the hut, the chanting was done. Some of the people
rested, curled in their bundles, but others milled about.

The blonde who'd lost her daughter leaned against her
white-haired husband. Her blouse was the color of the pájaro,
yellow and red, bright-breasted, wounded in the heart. The old
man's face had grown sharper, more aquiline.

"How are you?"

"All right."

I had eaten the bitter mash. It was bitter, but I had eaten
anyway. The bowl had come around the circle again, and I felt
the eyes of the others upon me. In the logic of the unfolding
moment, I dipped my fingers into the mash and put the bitter-
ness into my mouth. It was the same unfolding moment that had
led me from Coney Island to Omaha to here, to the Archuleta,
the instant under the desert sky where I'd glimpsed the thing
within, hidden from myself, already vanished, scampering into
the brush.

"Get some rest," the woman said. "There'll be the breakfast
when the sun comes up. Food trucks."

I found the jacket on the sleeping cot, my gun in its pocket.
Also, in another pocket, the keys to the ranch car we'd left in the
casino lot. The jacket was the rancher's, a goat-smelling thing

from the trunk of that squared-off sedan. The leather folio lay beneath. It smelled of dirt. I crawled to a far corner of the Quonset with a lithium torch. Inside the folio, I found a stained binder, loosely bound, files, some older than others, yellowing paper that likewise smelled of dirt, of animal droppings, a binder inside another binder stashed in a crawlspace under a migrant cabin visited by pocket mice and chuckwalla.

Pages fell out. Rolland's handwriting was large and careful, not difficult to read. It seemed I took in whole pages at a glance, but the words all tumbled away just as fast. Dated entries, projects, figures, names. An envelope, already opened, labeled on the outside:

For My Son, To Be Opened in The Event of My Death

Dear Zeke,

I have written this and written it again. Thrown the crumpled paper into the fire, watched my words turn to ash. Smoke rising over the malpais.

It is no secret, since your mother's death. My disgust with the Sundial Foundation,

With myself.

Never mind the usual veniality.

We allowed ourselves to go blind. Or to act as if we were blind. To the transgressions. Infiltration of money with origins in criminal sources.

I confronted the board. Only later to be informed—by government men——any action I might take, any foolishness.

Embedded agents. Working through proxy.

What they fear most of all, their own exposure, but that is a threat one dare not entertain.

Let alone speak.

· · ·

The letter went on, disjointed. Rolland had lost control of Sundial. Such organizations were permeable. The nature of the rules that allowed them to thrive—records shielded from public examination—made them attractive to outside influencers, foreign and domestic. They also drew the attention of government operatives, intelligence burrowing beneath the surface. Like vice cops on the street corner, undercover, working both sides of the ledger, the further they burrowed, the more entangled, the less they could afford exposure. Agent Moore wanted the folio. Was he trying to unearth that entanglement, or bury it? And where was his allegiance, to what superior, what subcommittee? Or just to himself?

There was more, other papers, more notes, shuffled, but not devoid of organization. Whatever Zeke had removed, I saw a pattern discernible in the papers that remained. Files clumped by project, attended by mission statements, correspondence, ledgers—marked with a highlighter and Mikel Rolland's notes.

For a moment it came unspeakably clear to me, the entire edifice, never mind how it shifted, changing shape in the peyote light. I grasped the underpinnings, the same as I had years before, leaning over the balcony at that fundraiser for the aspiring Gaddis. Maybe not the specifics, the details—I fumbled with the paper, shuffled, scanned—but I felt it in my body, a faint rumble in the breaking dawn. And then that clarity all slipped through my fingers onto the Quonset floor. I stooped to gather it back up.

The sun was rising, light slanting over the desert, shadows growing longer. A procession of vehicles rolled from the direction in which the jeep had taken flight. Men emerged, silhouettes in the half light, giant crows. I edged around the building toward the copse trail. I saw the Marquette anthropologist and her husband ahead, cheerful, transcendent, photographing the encampment in the growing dawn. I did not want to appear in their photo and dipped to the lower path. It was a long way back to the casino. I heard trampling. I had not zipped the folio, just slung its strap across my shoulder—a mistake, a hurried action—and felt the short nose weighting the jacket inside its pocket holster. I slid my hand in, fingered the safety. A shadow rose on the trail. The revolver pulled easily.

"Whoa! You! No!"

The paranoia hit me, the sun slanting hard. I dropped into the stance I had learned at the gun range in Sacramento. The man and his horse were a single entity, a dark figure rearing up. I didn't recognize the man at first—the older tribal cop, the peyote eater, out on a skittish horse, early morning patrol—but he reached across the saddle—for his gun, or just gathering the reins. I fired. Pulled past the safety. I didn't hit him, but the horse reared high, out of control—and a wild cry rang out behind me, echoing the gunshot, a high screaming noise that sounded to me like a spirit coming out of a rock. I whirled, shooting into the shadow. It was the woman from Marquette, looking at me with a startled expression. She dropped.

I had got her in the stomach.

Her husband stood a couple feet behind her. He should have turned and ran, but he didn't. He ran toward me.

I fired twice more.

I fell to my knees. I threw myself over into the canyon. The papers fell from the valise, tumbling as I scrabbled down the rocks. I saw myself as if from above, changing shape, getting smaller, first down one crevice, then another.

I hid in the drainage pipe at the bottom of the ravine.

Helicopters circled overhead.

Night came, and I clawed my way out of the ditch. There was no moon. I had swallowed it the night before. The helicopter beams didn't see me. I made my way along the shadow of the Archuleta, along the sandhills, coming out the back side of

Dulce, past the old wood frame houses and the trailer park. I became large, walking on two feet, but the night was so dark no one saw me. The dogs fell quiet as I went by. The Indians dimmed their porch lights.

I was my own size, my own spirit.

I kept to the backstreets, reaching the casino, the parking lot. Some cops stood on alert out front. The place inside would be abuzz, news on every wire. Maybe one of the cops looked at me, maybe he didn't, or maybe I was so ordinary as to be invisible, my true self still back in the desert, hiding in a crevice between the rocks. Whatever the truth, I pulled out of the casino lot headed west in the rancher's sedan, hallucinating as I drove down the road.

PART 7

LA BAHIA

TWENTY-NINE

September

I CAN'T ESCAPE the sensation I had after I fled Dulce, when the rancher's sedan broke down in the Mojave and I found myself seeking refuge in cave country. The feeling that I had always been here in the subterranean, and still am.

I walk the streets of La Bahia, a projection of that other self.

That creature lying on the cave floor... among the echoes and shadows... until those aging spelunkers stumbled upon me . . . ignorant of the radio reports....and pulled me to the surface.

I have not been La Bahia long, but I am already recognized around town, by the hangers-around: by the seat-tenders in the library, fishmongers at the wharf, the undercover cops who mingle with the homeless. La Costa, the company that owns the arcade—and much of the surrounding property (fenced lots, empty motels, cottages on the brink)—has is its own security people. Among these are that man in the yellow polo shirt I'd first seen not long after my arrival, standing in the doorway of the La Mosca café, watching the line of mourners snake their way through the Flats.

I've encountered him since.

Also, that young activist, the woman down at the wharf with her petitions, her earnest, distracted manner, her brown eyes that seem not to see me but to be gazing at some inner landscape.

Meanwhile, my situation at the La Bahia Hotel has grown tenuous. Technically we are all squatters, living under a vacate notice, but the termination date remains unknown, the authorities capricious, at odds with themselves. Public meetings are contentious, orders issued, rescinded, and in between these issuances and rescissions we get the police, random rousts, together with social service and city inspectors.

On the street one morning, I'm returning from the corner grocery, with a creeping chill in the air, a morning fog—when the cars gather. I retreat. In a day or two, the situation will revert. Until then, it's best to stay away, but not too long. Most of my money is in my room, hidden in the broken plaster in the lathing over the dresser, behind a picture of the sea. Robberies are common after the rousts; lockouts too. I taste the fog in the air. I am tempted to go back, rescue what I can, but I can't risk an encounter with the authorities. I am caught in between, nowhere to go. I head up the street, into that fog, and feel myself slipping into the permanent underground, that great wandering army that lives along the beach, in tents, under shrubs, in the beaten ground along the freeway.

I contemplated returning home: appearing suddenly in front of Renée, securing a lawyer, enlisting the help of people I had worked for—of Gaddis himself, whose secrets I know (some of them) and who has the power to bargain for me, to bring me back under the umbrella. Since my arrival, I'd been watching his campaign, looking for an opportunity. I considered, too, throwing myself at the mercy of Agent Moore and his anonymous friends.

But I wasn't ready to take that risk.

That red flare after Hite and Nunez took off— the black thunder in the canyon—had not been pure hallucination.

The plane had gone down.

According to the stories I'd read, contradictory as they may be, unverified.

I needed to get off the streets. I went to the bus station, with the idea of riding through the night, sleeping in anonymity, circling back—but I was overcome with homesickness and ended up outside my mother's nursing home in Napa.

A risk, too, if the place were under surveillance, but the home my sister had chosen was a small facility. Out of another time, it seemed. On a dead-end street, on a lot surrounded by yellowing palms.

Inside, my mother lay in a bed under a pile of blankets. Her face was skeletal, and the television was on. She shared the room with a woman who made indecipherable noises on the other side of the cloth. She recognized me by the sound of my footsteps.

"How was Manhattan?"

She moved back and forth in time. I did, too. Then, now.

"The city has changed. It's not what it used to be."

"Did you get your father his chicken?"

"I did."

She smiled mischievously.

"You were all over the news for a while. Then you weren't. Those stories—your suitcase in the gorge, your clothes. Then the rancher's car, two hundred miles away, your footsteps vanishing into the Mojave . . . No one comes out of that desert . . . Renée wants closure, the kids. But she needs a corpse, for that. Or a divorce."

"I'm not dead."

"You've been traveling."

"Some."

"It expands one's perspective."

"Are you comfortable?" I asked.

"A little cold, that's all. It's like a meat locker in here."

"Can I get you another blanket?"

I felt the chill, too. I'd felt it more lately, especially in the mornings, one needed warmth to get going.

"There aren't any more blankets. People here steal everything. My night clothes, my beautiful blouse."

This was true about nursing homes, I'd heard it more than once, the caretakers, they took your things.

"I guess they don't pay their employees very well."

"Even my ouroboro." She showed me her thin wrist. The silver bracelet was gone, the one she'd worn since Las Cruces, the serpent around the wrist, swallowing its own tail. "They take everything. I understand, the cycle of life, we consume ourselves to survive. God crawling out of Satan's ass . . ."

"Mom . . ."

"It's medical terminology. Don't be a prude. One gets older, one accepts reality. But the cold. Come here, get closer."

I got onto the bed. She was all bones under the blankets and clutched me close. I felt her shudder, pressed my bones against hers, and that shudder passed through my bones, too. I clutched her back, felt her lips touch the hollow of my shoulder, the wet spittle, each of us pressing close for the last bit of warmth.

She shuddered horribly.

The room grew dim.

I lay with my eyes open.

I am back in the cave, listening to the footsteps, the muttering.

The spelunkers leave me at the side of the road.

I lean my head against the Greyhound glass.

THIRTY

▭

THE WEATHER IN La Bahia shifted. It would shift back, according to the forecasters, but there remained a chill along the coast. In that chill, the city inspectors had descended upon the Hotel La Bahia. Time blurred, as time does. The raid had been day before last—a pair of nights, a long day in the middle, hours on the bus—so the authorities should be gone, and I needed to get back to claim my room.

I went up Pacific into the center of town. The fog hung on, but farther up the hill, toward the old mission, the sky lightened, and the sun shafted through. Downtown buzzed: café bums, locals in a rush, worn-out beach drifters, street performers, a tired man in dreads, an aging surfer—also families who'd taken the drive from the other side of the hill to escape the heat, ill-prepared for the sudden chill on the beach, sauntering around with too little clothing, bored, seeking refuge in the shops. The college, up on the plateau, was back in session, so students wandered among the rest, more so down in the plaza, by a flatbed campaign trailer hung with rainbow bunting, a bright banner:

Angela!

The Morales senate campaign had come to town. I'd had my eye on Gaddis, working the farther hustings. Morales had not been on my radar. The scene tugged at me, reminiscent of my old life, but plainclothes cops mingled among those waiting, and I needed to return to the La Bahia. A squad car blocked the usual way, and I went roundabout through the Flats, down jumbled barrio alleys under the shadow of the roller coaster. I was surprised at the number of people along the streets, many carrying signs, a crowd that thickened in front of a small church on the half-demolished street.

Angela Morales Para US Senate!
Get out La Costa! Ayuda Los Pobres!!
Save Our Neighborhood!!!

The crowd chattered among themselves. They'd come to hear Angela Morales speak in that church, but it was too full, overflowing. So, they planned to march with her through the streets to her rally at the flatbed. I meant to move on but was already in the midst of it. Behind me, a couple dozen yards—on-duty but cautious, keeping his distance—stood the man in the yellow polo shirt, the same man I'd seen at La Mosca when I'd first come to town, in the same outfit, a regular presence these days. Security after all, as it turned out, hired by La Costa Development. My initial impressions had been correct.

Meanwhile, motorcycle cops straddled their machines at the end of the block, and a patrolman emerged from a nearby alley. I edged away, deeper into the crowd. I spotted the petitioner, recognizing her by her bright, frayed hair—a halo about her head —and the clipboard held close to her chest.

She seemed delighted to see me.

Usually I bolted from her earnestness—but today I lingered, glad for the attention of someone within the crowd and the imagined protection.

"A supporter?"

"Just passing by."

"You know Angela's story."

"A little."

I knew more than that. Morales was a farmworker's daughter. Her father had walked with Cesar Chavez. She'd gone on scholarship to law school, worked as an attorney for the disenfranchised, served in the state legislature. Aside from the campaign biography, I knew other things as well, true or otherwise, that might cast her in less favorable light. *A pro bono client, farmworker accused of car theft . . . she'd helped acquit the man . . . . he was a runner for the Hernandez Cartel . . . whose organization funneled money to her first campaign.* Those half dozen phrases I'd sent months back, untraceable, through proxy server, to Eileen Watson, Gaddis's press monkey. She'd insisted, and I wanted the job.

"Angela needs your support. And we need her. All of us."

"What about them?"

I nodded toward the cops and the man in the polo shirt, the latter uncomfortable, nervous in his La Costa colors, the yellow shirt, the blue shorts. The cops appeared unconcerned, racking up their overtime, reinforcements in the wings.

"Bill," she said.

"You know his name?"

"He's not so bad."

The sympathy surprised me. She had no love for La Costa, who had bought half the Flats and surrounded it in chain link.

Their intention was to raze it all. The Morales campaign had come out in opposition to the new development. Gaddis stayed quiet, played the center. Whatever their differences, Gaddis and Morales didn't spar with each other. She was in a tighter election fight than he was—against an older, entrenched candidate—and for this reason her race got more attention. She also generated more passion from the grassroots, more national media. Rumor was, if she survived this election, she'd speak at the party's national convention. *The Times* had just run an article on her growing support: an emerging figure, a threat to Gaddis not now, but later, inside his own party.

It was the kind of nascent internecine party rivalry that the press relished. And loved to stir.

But *The Times* didn't know, not yet, what Eileen Watson knew: information which—if properly handled, properly timed—would put a ceiling on Morales' rise.

Watson might not play that card now. The party could use Morales in the senate.

But later . . .

The street crowd thickened. A couple of burly men guarded the front, keeping onlookers off the sagging porch. The applause carried. So did Morales's amplified voice—audible but not quite comprehensible—mixed with the squalling gulls: *Dear people, nuestro barrio.* Words lost in the ocean sounds, the careening coaster. *¡No más niños hambrientos!* A brief thunder of applause.

The young activist's eyes grew wide. *¡Yo trabajo para ti!* I'd seen her around town often—not just at the foot of the wharf, but at the grocery, on the mall, always with her petitions. There was familiarity between us. She was the type campaigns like this depended on, true believers, unpaid, who would canvas every hovel.

"You don't have to worry about him."

"Who?

"Bill—from La Costa. He's with their security crew, shift manager. I volunteer at the shelter, and he's brought people to us, instead of calling the cops. So, he's not so bad. But his employer . . ." She shook her head, her voice grew winsome. "He needs the job, the work. Recently divorced. His thing, he likes to play volleyball at the beach."

Her assessment didn't reassure me. Okay, the guy chummed both sides—the cops, social services—but it didn't mean he could be trusted. If my face showed on the scan—if there was a match on some random camera—he'd turn me in.

The doors swung wide, people bumping out, the big men clearing a way. Angela wouldn't appear for a bit, but the street crowd crushed forward, wanting a glimpse, blocking those who pushed from the other direction, trying to leave. The push and the pull created a crosscurrent, an undertow that oscillated back through the crowd.

"What's your name?"

"Sam," I lied.

I grew wary of her, the same wariness I'd felt before, of her idealism, the wholesome fervor.

"If people would resist, fight back. Or just think about the consequences of their actions."

"Yes."

"It's intolerable what we do in the name of survival. The lies we tell ourselves."

I heard a thin whir overhead, swooping low, a security drone. Behind us, a television reporter worked the crowd, a local station with a national feed. The petitioner touched my shoulder, then reached into her briefcase, with its million petitions. I clutched her sleeve a moment, jostled backwards in the surge.

The drone hovered, moved on.

"I'm not registered."

"You don't have to be. Not for this one. All I need is a name, a local address."

It was a petition for saving the La Bahia.

Her eyes beseeched me, vulnerable, bright. Her face was such, her expression—refulgent in its naivete—that I at once wanted to reach out to touch her and to bat her away.

"I'm just passing through."

"It doesn't matter for this petition. Even if you're homeless, if you live on the beach, you can put down the shelter as your address."

"I'm not from around here."

"You live in the La Bahia Hotel."

"No."

"I've seen you."

She took me by the arm. The crowd buffeted.

"March with us."

I saw this would be a victory for her, to get someone out of the community into the parade. I was tempted. I felt the tug. This might be a way back for me, not to where I'd been, but someplace new, luminous. I wondered where she lived, the view out her window, if her curtains were the color of her skirt. The television reporter drew close.

Angela Morales appeared in the doorway. Angela the Good. Who, in her goodness, might be willing to help me in exchange for certain information. Or make the pretense. Except she wasn't that good. Also, she had no real power.

The crowd ebbed forward, drawing the petitioner in tow.

I pulled away.

"Come," she said.

I shook my head. Angela Morales wasn't going to help me. I was better off with the devil I knew.

THIRTY-ONE

AT FIRST GLANCE, the La Bahia lay in its usual somnolence. There were the familiar vagrants out front, the same yellowing signs on the door, the expired vacant notice, a demolition permit whose date had come and gone. Inside the situation was more dire. A line of dispossessed tenants stretched away from the manager's office, and untended possessions lay scattered about the courtyard. I found my room padlocked. Across the hall, the old woman who lived there, her door stood open. Her name was Minnie, and I caught a glimpse of her in her pink blouse and white shorts. Her legs were long and thin—too thin. She had trouble getting downstairs and spent most of her time in her room with her dog, a tiny creature with enormous eyes. The animal lay on the floor curled in front of a rotating fan.

"What happened?"

"You better go downstairs." She held a scold in her eyes. We hadn't spoken for a while, since before the disruption, when I'd gone to the store to pick up a few things—ice for her, gin, a can of

La Petite for the dog—but failed to return. "You better go stand in line."

The manager seemed in no hurry. He was assisted by a motorcycle mechanic who'd once ridden with the Gypsy Jokers and now worked maintenance for the hotel, a job involving little maintenance in the usual sense, but rather standing by in situations such as this, monkey wrench in hand. The manager had no waiting list, no rate card. Whatever hierarchy existed—who must go, who might stay, and at what cost—changed each time the city executed one of its raids.

At the front of the line, a hapless man made his case, but grew too persistent, too loud, and the manager lost patience.

"There's nothing I can do. Your room, such a pigsty. Bed bugs, lice, shitty toilet, it's in no condition for humans. The city insists." He directed his disgust down the line. "They shut a dozen rooms, uninhabitable. What am I supposed to do?"

The tenants bowed their heads. After every raid, his rant was the same. The city was cracking down. He had no choice but to keep squatters out. "The wrecking ball is coming, if not this week, then next. So, count yourself lucky." The manager changed his tone, speaking more slowly and carefully, condescending, as if trying to impart common sense to children.

"This is life. One door opens, another closes."

Everyone understood the situation. The La Bahia was his fiefdom. By what arrangement, by whose grace, everyone knew better than to inquire. He determined the currency and value of the coin. He replaced the dispossessed with those higher on their luck: petty thieves who'd secured a fence, dealers who paid a percentage, women who knew the score—and people like me, drifters of unknown origin who had the ability to pay cash but the inability to go elsewhere. He held a residual favoritism for old-timers and those on disability, especially those with caseworkers, because he did not want backlash from social services.

The line diminished slowly. One by one, they argued, they cajoled. The fortunate, by whatever whispered arrangement, made it back to their rooms. The others were escorted by the mechanic, together with their belongings, out into the street.

My turn came.

"My door is padlocked."

"Your floor, that side of the building—the corner room especially, visible from the street—it needs to be vacated."

"Why?"

"Windows are the eyes to the soul," the manager said. "People see light inside, they think something's going on. It is an embarrassment to the City Inspector, this flagrant violation."

"What about the old woman?"

"You want I should throw her into the street?"

"That's not . . ."

"She lives alone with that dog, an interior apartment—a woman with a name, with Social Security. You, I don't even have a name to give the city. The city, they need names. Social services, the cops, they need names. No name, you don't exist. You live on the street."

"We had an arrangement."

"Your place, with a view of the ocean, secure, three floors up, it's desirable."

He wrote down a number.

"That's too much."

"Then go somewhere else."

He knew I couldn't. I was on the down low, and the other hotels required identification. He had me in a bind. I had enough cash on me to pay him, but most of my money was upstairs, tucked behind the slats in the broken plaster. I could not retrieve it if I did not pull out my wallet for him now.

"Two weeks," I said.

"One."

"This isn't right."

"Things have changed. I have expenses, too—and it isn't just me. There are people, every inch along the way, who need their piece to keep this place safe. Anyway, I can't guarantee two weeks. The wrecking crew, the crane—the dynamite, how long? Who can say?"

I paid.

The mechanic took me up and undid the padlock. He had a peace sign for a tattoo, also a swastika. My room had been rummaged, nothing subtle about it: the skewed mattress, open drawers, clothes and belongings scattered. The picture of the sea, covering the broken plaster over the bureau, hung aslant.

"City inspectors," the mechanic said. "Gangsters. Communists. They have no respect."

He shrugged.

This happened. Thieves, opportunists, working in the backwash of the inspection, foraging for loot. Insiders, too, like the mechanic himself.

He shrugged again.

The old woman came to gander, spraddle-legged in the doorway. She held a drink in one hand, in a tall blue glass. I asked after her dog.

"How's Little Mister?"

"He's fine."

"You got yourself some ice."

"My caseworker went down for me."

"That was thoughtful."

"Government workers," she shrugged, unimpressed. "They do anything for a little pussy."

She went back to Little Mister. I shut the door and lifted the picture from the wall. I reached behind the broken slats, looking for the money I'd stashed. I broke away the plaster, then broke away some more. I pulled the shade off the lamp and angled the light into the crevice. I looked in the drawers. I rummaged through the pile of my clothes and scattered belongings. They'd taken my stiletto knife, too, the one I'd used to survive in the cave, skinning small animals. Leaving me with little enough. Frayed beach shirts on the closet floor, Sunglass under the bed. Pants I'd last worn in the desert, crumbled in the corner, pockets creased with sand.

THIRTY-TWO

▭

THE HEAT IS back. The onshore flow never reaches the shore, and the low bank of fog stays off on the horizon, over the ocean, its size diminishing each day until finally it isn't there at all and the day breaks with the sun flaming up out of the east. The heat from the interior settles back over the La Bahia, a blank and cloudless sky, yet blanker and emptier. The ocean seems to be rolling away from us, retreating, the low tide leaving a wider beach, so in the afternoon, before the tide creeps back, the sea is a like a mirage in the distance, shimmering at the edge of the sand.

Seagulls wilt off the cliffs, and sand crabs skitter apart at the seams, desiccating in the dry kelp. The crowds, already diminished in the wake of tourist season, diminish yet further, and those who remain—who can no longer stand the stink of their hotel rooms—seek refuge along the boardwalk, under the awnings of the arcade.

I seek refuge there as well.

I watch them stroll by—the local teenagers, the girls in their halters, the young families, kids sucking flavored ice, all ambling from one end to the other, gazing at the amusement rides, as if there might be some relief in those whirligigs.

La Costa has hired more security, more men and women in yellow polo shirts. I should be moving along, but I feel safe behind my shades, as if I can see without being seen, as if I am invisible. I watch a family pass by, a handsome woman, a beautiful husband, two wide-eyed children. I feel a sudden disquietude, an insatiable hunger. The way the woman moves, so thoughtless in her sundress, how the man touches her arm, the utter fidelity of the kids at their heels, I want to devour them whole.

THIRTY-THREE

GADDIS AND HIS Big Blue Bus were on their way to Salinas. I'd seen the posters around town and in the depot. I'd been on campaign buses and knew what that entailed: the tight sleeping bunks, the sloshing toilet at the back, the campaign staff around a Formica table, bumping knees with the press corps, the chosen ones. These days, few people, especially the candidate, stayed on the bus for long. There were nicer places to sleep, to eat—hosted by contributors—and limousines ferried the candidate to catch up with the bus outside the next town ahead. This leg had started in Atascadero, then gone through King City, Soledad, Paso Robles, its last stop scheduled for this afternoon in Salinas. Then, if what I'd heard discussed at his dinner held true, Gaddis would take a break with Candice at their place down the coast.

If things had gone differently, I might have been with him, a member of the entourage. I still entertained the thought that Gaddis might be willing to help me. If not out of goodness, then fear. Because what I didn't know, I could surmise—the path of laundered money, third-party donations, investment property transferred to his blind trust via an LLC. That surmisal, right or wrong, even if he dodged it now . . .

These matters had a way of boomeranging, details accruing, taking on a life of their own, catching you from behind.

More immediately, I needed to risk an ATM. Not in La Bahia, it was too close. I got off at the Salinas station and headed to the city's Chinatown, past the warehouses along the tracks, a tent city in the hollow, barred cottages, old temples, scavenger shops, a rescue mission. The neighborhood was mostly Mexican now, and along the main street the Advocacy Center had filled a storefront with pictures of immigrant children at the border. I went into a store with an ATM sign in the window. The machine was near the cashier: an older, third-party machine with lower limits but which relied upon the store's security as opposed to the embedded devices at the banks. The transaction would not go directly into the corporate mainframe, so there might be more of a delay before I could be traced. But I did not know this for sure: whether the account had been discovered and flagged—left open as bait, to pin my location—or simply closed altogether. I hadn't used it since Bakersfield.

The machine processed slowly.

The cashier watched.

The machine paused.

It flashed questions in yellow type.

It flashed more.

The money came, but there was a daily limit. I'd have to come back later for more cash, after midnight.

I approached the counter for cigarettes. I was an unfamiliar face, white, and the counter woman regarded me curiously. She went slowly for the cigarettes, achingly so. She reached and fiddled. Handbills advertising a massage parlor in several languages rested on the counter. I glanced down at them. The woman saw my glance. When I paid, she inclined her head toward the street.

"You want girl for afternoon."

I shook my head.

"Smart. You better off buying one. Boy, girl—they bring up from border in cage. You keep for yourself or rent out. Business opportunity."

She winked.

I walked past the Advocacy Center, with its lost children in the window. The door was open, and a man stood behind the counter.

▭

A GROUP OF party loyalists gathered about the Big Blue Bus on Old Main, a welcoming committee, I thought, then realized no, the energy was wrong; all but the hard-core had wandered off. I wanted a chance at Gaddis (who knew people in Justice—who always had, even back then—cohorts leaning over those high balconies, mutual interests to protect) but I'd misplayed my hand. The bus had pulled in ahead of schedule for an impromptu lunch at a downtown cafe where the candidate would sit with the locals, eat the World-Famous Salinas Chili— then work the street. These impromptus, I knew, were not as impromptu as all that; arranged by district reps, leaked out to party regulars and friends in the press. Now Gaddis stood, the Big Blue Bus behind him, indefatigable in his shirt sleeves, answering questions from reporters, his limo idling on the curb just ahead. I edged toward the press circle, but too late. Gaddis was done, eyes roaming the periphery of the remaining crowd— and his eyes met mine. Or I thought they did. I felt their soft gaze —those sincere, penetrating eyes—and felt, too, that small shiver shake my body, the one the best candidates could communicate, even if in reality they had not seen you at all.

The press wanted more, but an aide stepped between them and the limo, a long-armed man accomplished at such maneuvers.

"Sorry, folks, so sorry. The lieutenant governor must be on his way."

I darted around the ring toward the limo, but a man blocked me: campaign security in plain clothes.

"Gaddis and I have an appointment," I said. "He's expecting me."

The man didn't believe the lie, or if he did, it didn't matter. A woman intervened, a campaign aide with a softer approach, not wanting a scene—making pretense, at least, of determining who I might be. This didn't matter either. Gaddis was already in the car, Candice beside him, the limo pulling from the curb.

THIRTY-FOUR

I went with my burner phone into an artichoke field east of town. The artichokes were high, and the field stretched toward the white hills at the edge of the valley. I walked along a drainage culvert away from the workers and the harvesting machines. I dialed the number on the card Agent Moore had handed me in the perpetual twilight of that motel in the Canal.

The line rang through.

They could ping my location, I figured, or a close approximation, triangulating from the cell towers in the vicinity.

"Moore," he said.

"Agent Moore?"

"Who's speaking?"

I'd been through this in my head, the logic of it. I'd called the number before but never gotten to this point. Either because I'd hung up, losing my nerve, or because the phone had rung endlessly before flipping into a silence punctuated by a slow clicking, a steady pulse, that I imagined to be the network tracking my location. Unless I spoke, identifying myself, they had no reason to follow the ping.

"We met in San Rafael. You and I and one of your colleagues —in a motel room down by the Canal."

He didn't say anything right away, but I'd given him enough. Too much. My doubts returned. I should have stuck with Gaddis.

"You've been lying low."

Moore sounded irritated, as if I had caught him in the middle of something else.

"You know where I am?"

"That's right," he said. "Just waiting for your call. All our technical resources on tap, so we can zero in on you at any second. Important national emergency like yourself."

His voice held the same irony, feigned or otherwise, that I'd heard during our last meeting. I still wondered about the affiliation of his colleague, and about Moore, too. I'd checked the Federal Building in San Francisco, where there was an Agent Moore, though with a different phone number: a line picked up by an assistant who'd told me that Agent Moore spent a lot of time in the field, but would give me a call, if I left my number. I hadn't. I wondered about this Moore and that Moore, if they were the same man.

"You told me to call," I said.

"You took your time."

"I caught up with Valerie Hite, in Dulce, with the Apache." Most of the stories I'd read reported that the plane had gone down not long after takeoff, an engine fire, killing the pilot and two others, all fleeing federal warrants. Some locals claimed the explosion had been sabotage, a timer planted by the Feds. "I got caught in a firefight at the scene, and his papers were scattered all over the arroyo. Your people were there."

"My people?"

"You're all related, aren't you?"

It was hard for me to imagine that the sudden appearance of the dawn caravan—accompanied by all those initialed operatives —had been coincidental. Or that they hadn't examined the scene afterwards. But maybe it had been as reported, a dawn raid aimed at Apache outlaws smuggling people and drugs using the tribal airstrips, and the fleeing plane had gone down unexpectedly over the desert.

"What's this about?"

"The shooting in Dulce, New Mexico," I said. "The press reports, they have me missing. Or dead."

"Do you really want to change that?"

I let it sit there, unsure how to respond.

"Come in. We can have you debriefed. We can put you in witness protection."

"I know some influential people."

"Of course, you do."

"What if I go public?"

"With what?"

I fell silent. The silence went on, with that vague hissing in the background. I could not tell if the hissing came from the cell. There were some gulls overhead, a scampering in the dirt, the whirring of irrigation wheels, the workers feeding the harvesting wagon, tossing the artichokes into the rattling conveyor. The little tractor, far off, veered around, heading in my direction. The ocean blurred into that shining horizon. The oil derricks were sketched on the water, cars swooshing by on the gray ribbon, a kid flying a drone in the motel parking lot on the other side of the road. A truck yanked into the roadside gravel behind. The little man on the tractor grew bigger, moving toward me. I was on foot. The call had been a mistake. All I wanted was to make a deal. Forget about me, and I'll forget about you.

"I want my life back."

The line was dead.

There was no one to debate with, no one to convince. The harvesting machine turned at the end of the row, back the way it had come, the tractor, too. They grew distant under the sun. The sky overhead was empty. I walked to the edge of the field, past the man sitting in his truck. He talked on his phone, just talking, not minding me. I walked through Chinatown toward the depot, past the massage parlors. I wanted more from the ATM but needed to wait until the clock rolled over, resetting the limit. I loitered till midnight. The Advocacy Center lay dark, all those children in the window.

I walked past them into Lin's All-Night Magic Grocery.

The machine took the same forever.

I studied the slot, waiting. A drunk entered the store, an old drunk. I got some more money from the ATM and took the milk run home.

THIRTY-FIVE

SOMEONE HAD COME to visit while I was gone. According to Minnie. Who had heard footsteps in the hall. But there were always footsteps, wanderers twisting door handles, transients. I got out scissors and soap and a fresh razor. There was no warm water, no shower, so I used cold from the tap and lathered with a washrag. I shaved off the fledgling beard, trimmed my hair, regarded the mirror. Then scrubbed myself again. The ceiling fan had stopped working. The effort of toweling myself worked up a sweat. My face was ruddy, chafed from the sun, creased around the eyes; and my skin leathery, sloughing and peeling at the back of my neck, itchy, forming tiny scales that fell away when I touched. I had picked up some clothes downtown, paying cash: a white shirt and tan slacks, new shoes, lightweight clothing—the sort of casual stuff I wore to client meetings when it was time to roll up the sleeves—but the shirt was already damp beneath the arms.

I reconsidered approaching Gaddis. If I did so neatly

dressed, clear-eyed, better prepared, perhaps I'd have better luck. It wasn't possible to get to his place down the coast by bus. I'd checked with the rental outfit on Portola about reserving a car, but they'd need a license and a bank card. It meant further risk. I didn't know if Gaddis had recognized me in Salinas, or if I'd get past his security at the beach house. I knew he liked to jog in the morning, to take long runs along the sand at the tidal edge. I could try to catch him down there.

I wanted to go home, and allowed myself to imagine Renée at the door, the kids—the infinity pool, our house at the foot of the hill—the monarchs bursting from their dark pupas into the light.

The old woman, Minnie, milled around in her room, door open, and caught sight of me stepping out. She squinted, giving me the once over.

"What are you doing?"

"I have to run some errands."

"You are all cleaned up." She took a step closer. "All new clothes." Her admiration made me uneasy. "You're leaving us soon. You're moving out."

"No," I lied.

I didn't want the attention. The downtown rental counter closed early. I didn't have another place to stay this evening and could not afford to have the manager pull the rug. I carried all my cash—not intending to make the same mistake twice—but left my few other belongings in the room.

"Just going out for a quick bite."

"That's what they always say. A quick bite. But, you know— this place, it's not so easy to escape. I've seen it, people get lost before they even get out of the building." As fearful as she might be of the street, she didn't want to be stuck here either. "I don't know what I'm going to do."

"I'll be back. Do you want anything?"

"No, I don't eat anymore." She nodded at her dog. "Something for him, maybe. Fiesta La Petite. A little can."

"Of course."

Little Mister lay on the floor, eyes traveling from one of us to the other, hot and miserable, no matter the fan blowing over the bowl of ice water she'd positioned in front of him to imitate the effect of a breeze over a cool lake.

"He has trouble with his sweat glands, you know."

The dog understood we were talking about him. He turned away as if embarrassed at his existence, at his enormous eyes, his unpleasant hide, hideously textured, the color of an old rag. He fidgeted, squirming, uncomfortable in the body in which he was trapped, skin stretched tightly over his bones.

"Poor thing," I said.

"A pint of gin, if you can remember." She smiled in her pink blouse. "Who do you think you are?"

"I'll be right back."

"You belong on TV."

"I do."

"This is an historical building. They wouldn't dare tear this place down."

Maybe Minnie was right. Maybe the La Bahia was immune from the wrecking ball. But right or wrong, wrecking ball or no, sooner or later management took your corporal self, living or dead, and threw it into the street. Little Mister whined, a tiny yelp. He turned in a circle, trying to get comfortable. I could see his misery. He might be better off if I stepped into the room and smothered him with the chair cushion. Minnie too. She wore her pink blouse unbuttoned one too many buttons. I had a number of ugly thoughts; not mine, I told myself—these thoughts came from elsewhere. I couldn't afford to entertain them. I had errands to run. I passed the manager on the way out, sleeping under the banana tree in the courtyard; also, an overweight man on the corner, elephantine in his white shorts; a disgruntled blonde; a small person of indeterminate sex; a good-looking Mexican boy who looked as if he wanted to stab me; people I'd passed hundreds of times in the last few weeks. None of them seemed to recognize me.

This filled me with a small ebullience. I'd been haunted by the notion I was being followed, but perhaps what Agent Moore had told me way back in the motel was true. So long as I didn't exist, I didn't matter. No one gave a shit about me.

Meanwhile, I needed sundries. Some deodorant, to get the stink out. Fresh underwear. Jogging shorts. A small traveler's case.

I got most of what I needed at a sportswear shop downtown and the traveler's case from the office end of the local bookstore, behind the beach towels and refrigerator magnets. I had doubts about the wisdom of returning to the La Bahia, so I dipped into a place by the depot: old folks in the lobby, heads leaning against the wall—but the clerk needed a week in advance and the usual identification.

A gray sedan drove by.

It meant nothing, there were a million gray sedans. The old chill descended on me, accompanied by that sharp yearning— for a drink, for the road home, for some lost life. In this mood, I had little desire to return to my stifling room at the hotel. I bought the old lady's gin (her brand, anyway) and got a cup of ice at the arcade. I milled among the people there, the scent of warm bodies, the lotion. It all stirred a longing—and then I wandered across the trestle, a drink in one hand, my traveling case in the other. The beach widened below: kids clobbering a whiffle ball, hitting fungoes with an aluminum bat, volley-ballers, net staked in the sand. The sun dropped, casting a white flare over the sea. I picked my way down the cliff. Up coast, along the more rugged beaches, the homeless had their encampments, but this was a neighborhood beach, stairs up to the street at the farther end that led to a crumbling road lined with eucalyptus.

I sat on driftwood and poured gin into the plastic cup. I felt foolish, sitting in my dress clothes. I had nowhere to go. If I went home, the risk was too great, not just for me . . . But . . . If I appeared on Gaddis's beach, how would that be, waiting for him to appear, moving toward him in my running shorts and sleeveless shirt along the water's edge . . . . His wife Candice might be with him, some campaign aide . . . He would balk at the sight of me. I didn't fit in his narrative. He would find it better to turn me in . I would have to wrestle him to the ground, shove his face in the sand.

A suit . . . a blurred face in a photo. . . . with his own fear of the Feds.

A pawn.

In a game where the criminals and the enforcers and everyday fools loll around in the same bed but pretend otherwise. Never mind the scattered folio, the shifting players, illusive rules. Everybody knows.

The only crime was to talk about it.

I finished the drink, contemplated another. The ice was gone. Gazing across the sand, I recognized one of the volleyballers: the man in the yellow polo—only off duty now, out of uniform, in swimming trunks and a bright tee, dark shades. The man was good at the game, a bit clumsy but watchful, almost lithe. The woman playing next to him seemed to enjoy his presence. He fed, she spiked. In a while, it would be too dark to play, but they kept at it. Between sets, he retreated to the grill. The woman joined him. The sun spiraled down, and I poured myself more gin. The ball got away from the players and rolled to where

I sat, and he came running to retrieve it and glanced into my face. If he recognized me, he gave no sign.

He trotted back to the group, and I was filled with rage. I don't know why. It might have been the impersonal nature of his look. Because in the end he didn't know who I was. Or pretended he didn't. I felt the net tightening. There was the smell of the grill, and the sound of the game, and the ocean thrumming. Down the beach, couples gathered their towels, families trudged through the sand, headed home. I envied them. The impossibility of my situation overcame me.

The volleyballers started to break up. He stayed behind— talking with that same woman, and I saw there wasn't quite anything between them, not yet, but there would be. The kids had dropped their bat and were busy in the dying light, poking at a seal carcass down along the tide. The young woman left, together with a friend, but not before giving a last look back. The man caught the look. He stayed behind with a couple of sunburned others, stumbling dregs, who gathered up the net and left him alone to finish his beer and regard the sunset. He picked up his cooler, dumped the ice onto the fire, and put the empty beer cans into his duffle, along with a couple volley-balls. He gave me a glance, checked his phone. He hesitated, then slid the device in his pocket. I wondered about the hesita-tion. I gathered up the bat the kids had left behind. They danced on the seal. My man lagged well behind the rest of them. It was a long trudge across the sand toward the staircase up the cliff. I had the angle on him and was less encumbered, with only the traveling case slung over my shoulder and the aluminum bat to carry. I finished off my drink and threw the cup into the sand.

"Beautiful night," I said.

"Yes," he said. "If you like the heat."

"You left this behind, I think."

He looked at the bat, then me. Something passed over his face.

"No, I don't think so. Maybe those kids."

"You're pretty weighed down. Let me grab something there."

"There's no need."

"It's a hard climb," I said.

My persistence perturbed him. Cataloguing the street people in his head, trying to place me. I could have backed off then—but he'd gotten a good look. I'd exposed myself. There were video cameras everywhere, facial recognition software, a phone in his pocket. He would put it together, if he hadn't already. I followed him up the long stairs. He started to weave, bending under the weight of the cooler on one side and the bag of volleyballs over his back.

"Exhausting," I said.

"I'm okay."

We were at the top of the stairs. It was all but dark.

For an instant I felt sorry for him. He was not even a cop, just a security guard, someone who wandered around the properties, gathered information, took pictures, compiled reports. Dispatched them here, there. Adjusted facts, according to the needs of the situation, of his employers. Divorced, according to the petitioner. Regretting the life he'd ruined, maybe, yearning for another, doing what he could to get by. A familiar creature. I recognized him, even if he didn't recognize me. He craned his neck, sensing me behind him—a dawning realization, prickling at his collar—and set down the cooler. He stood up and I came around with the bat. I hit him and his head whipsawed back.

His fingers let go the bag as he fell. The balls tumbled loose.

He dropped to his knees, and I hit him again.

I heard the skull crack.

The night carried the slightest chill. There was the sound of the waves. The smell of marijuana. Shadows in the eucalyptus.

I dragged the bat through the dusk and threw it in the ocean.

I stumbled along the sand. I felt vulnerable out in the open. I could not see so well in the dark. The gulls cawed. Though the air was warm, it was not warm enough. The cold gripped me from within. I found shelter in the ice plants, in the space between the rocks.

I know who I am.

THIRTY-SIX

▭

I CAME UP from the other side of the wharf and emerged within sight of the arcade and the La Bahia and the tin-roofed cabana at the end of the pier. The activist sat where I'd first met her, several weeks back.

"What happened to you?"

"I had places to be."

She took this as meaning that I'd joined the great masses and been sleeping under bridges. She didn't know who I had been, once upon a time. My cards were still good, I told myself. I could still make my way to the rental counter. I could wend my way over the hills, back to my old life.

I closed my eyes.

The sun kissed my face. It parched my lips and sucked the breath out of me. The woman leaned close. I could see her earnestness.

She ordered beer, food—a little calamari for sharing. Men watched from the bar. Plainclothes, maybe.

A gray sedan sat empty down the way.

"What are you going to do?"

"I have an appointment."

"Everything depends on people like us," she said. "We can't give in."

I understood what was coming next. She started to talk, the long talk, that of the true believer—that stuff about the long arc of justice, that business about the meek—and I saw the light in her eye. I put my hand on her shoulder.

She looked up at me, full of hope.

"I have to go," I said.

THIRTY-SEVEN

▭

THE COURTYARD IS empty, except for the banana tree. The manager's door stands open on the next floor. I hear the voices, the whispering and the footsteps—nothing, really, my own footfalls—as I head up the wooden staircase to my room. The old woman's door stands open as well. I have come back empty-handed again, no gin, no Fiesta La Petite. I put the key in the latch bolt, but it's already been thrown, and the knob turns easily in my hand. I turn to Minnie. She raises a finger to her lips, shushing me, and pushes her own door shut. I walk into my room. A noose hangs from the rafters, carefully knotted, a bright plastic chair positioned below. Standing on the chair, you can see over the boardwalk to the sea. You can hear the roller coaster, the cries and the laughter, the rolling of the cars up and down the tracks, and the footsteps in the hall, the creaking of the La Bahia.

I can see the wrecking crane, and—on this hot and glimmering day—the shine off the ocean, those gray oil derricks way out there in the bay.

I put my hands on the noose.

I peer through it to the sea.

A gull swoops by.

I close my eyes and peer deeper. The world is not inviolable. It can be penetrated, and will be, a trigger pulled, a flame ignited. I feel the breeze tremble through the window, smoke (wildfire, outside my mother's house, my father's, closer now, the hills forever in flame). I am here, and I am there, too. Back in the cave, imagining myself in this other life, dreaming it up. I work for Gaddis, or the Antichrist (the one with the orange hair), or Her Majesty's Secret Service. They study me, eyes slitted, though all this time we have shared the same cave. I have my job back, my family, the sweet smell of that lost life, not lost. Back in the cave, my existence depends on what happens up here—on the heat I generate, the story I tell—and I feel the chill creeping into my bones.

I am frightened, I have ceased to sweat. I hear the whispers on my drying tongue, the footsteps approaching from behind.

The spelunkers boost me toward the shaft. I resist at first. They cinch my neck, waist, my feet, lift beneath the shoulders. It is a long way out, up through the lava tubes. The shaft narrows. I flatten my chest tight to the rock, wriggle. The rope burns. I claw, feet dangling. Flail for purchase. The spelunkers yank and push, the last bit, wrenching me onto the surface.

An impossible passage.

I blink away the light, blink again. My skin thickens, eyes narrow.

All but transformed.

On the flats outside Bakersfield, old Highway 99, I dangle my thumb out in the heat. Or something that once resembled my thumb.

No one stops.

The drivers have heard the news, the shootings in the desert. The sun descends. Nearby, the ground is barren, but there are houses off in the distance. The crows hover. I skitter under the guardrail and lie down, my belly on the warm rocks by the side of the road. I peer out.

ACKNOWLEDGMENTS

Special thanks to my wife, poet and editor Gillian Conoley—and to maverick editors Kurt Lipshutz and Jim Thomsen—who read this manuscript in its various stages and were ruthless in their support of its underlying vision, but of course bear no fault for its shortcomings. Also, to Gillis, who listened to music with me in the car.

DOMENIC STANSBERRY is a crime novelist, editor and essayist primarily known for his innovative noir fiction that skirts the edges of the genre while exploring the intricacies of criminal consciousness. Among his recent books is *The White Devil*, a sultry, decadent thriller that received the Hammett Prize from the International Association of Crime Writers. An earlier novel, *The Confession*, received the Edgar Award from the Mystery Writers of America in 2005, and is regarded as a neo-noir classic. Other work includes the North Beach Mystery Series—featuring investigator Dante Mancuso — which received wide praise for its portrayal of the ethnic and political subcultures of San Francisco. Books from that series include *The Ancient Rain*, named several years after its original publication as one of the best crime novels of the decade by *Booklist*. Stansberry's novels have been translated into numerous languages, with editions in Japanese, Italian, French, Spanish and Polish among others. He lives with his wife, poet Gillian Conoley, in a small town north of San Francisco.

Photo: Gillian Conoley

The White Devil

The Confession

Chasing The Dragon

The Big Boom

Ancient Rain

Naked Moon

Chasing the Dragon

Manifesto for the Dead

The Last Days of Il Duce

The Spoiler

Exit Paradise

The Infamous Murder Kit Trilogy

THE LIZARD: A former investigative reporter—a man of multiple identities, now working as a political ghostwriter— is thrust into the center of a conspiracy investigation after an illicit romance turns deadly. Part political thriller, part expressionist nightmare: a timely contemporary tale of betrayal, murder and violent transformation, laced with the author's signature black humor.

———

THE CONFESSION: This neo-noir thriller tells the story of a forensic psychologist accused of strangling his mistress—and does so through the unnerving, charming, intelligent, often unreliable voice of the accused himself. This **Edgar Award**

winning novel helped establish Stansberry's reputation as a master of the psychological noir.

—

THE WHITE DEVIL: A sparse, chilling tale of a young American actress—alleged adulteress and murderer—living in the ex-patriot community in Rome. Together with her charming but troublesome brother, the young woman finds herself implicated in a series of crimes dating back to her childhood. *Winner of* **Hammett Prize** *for Literary Excellence in Crime Fiction.*

—

IN TRADE PAPER AND E-BOOK
AVAILABLE EVERYWHERE FROM
MOLOTOV EDITIONS

THE LIZARD BY DOMENIC STANSBERRY
#978-1-948596-05-3 $18.95 PAPER

THE CONFESSION BY DOMENIC STANSBERRY #978-1-948596-02-2 $16.95 PAPER

THE WHITE DEVIL BY DOMENIC STANSBERRY
#978-0-9967659-1-6 $, 15.95 PAPER

www.molotoveditions.com

www.ingramcontent.com/pod-product-compliance
Lightning Source LLC
Chambersburg PA
CBHW061756190726
48289CB00007B/1973